ARTHUR KING

AND THE CURIOUS CASE OF THE
TIME TRAIN

"The Ghost Train legend is from the era that Holmes first appeared in the *Strand Magazine*. It's fate that we should realize who we are meant to be just as the Ghost Train returns. Arthur, we have a mystery to solve."

"Yes, and as soon as I prove that Mr Toppol is a pervert, unfit to teach in this school, we shall solve that mystery. Hmm, I shall put him under surveillance."

"No, Arthur, Mr Toppol doesn't enter into this. It's the Ghost Train that's the mystery."

"Then he's something to do with that very mystery and I shall not rest until I implicate him in the dire plot. Whatever that dire plot is, of course. Until the striking of the lunch-bell, Watson," said Arthur in his best upper-class English accent, striding proudly into school.

Look out for Arthur's first adventure:

THE LEGEND OF
ARTHUR KING

ARTHUR KING

AND THE CURIOUS CASE OF THE
TIME TRAIN

DEAN WILKINSON

■SCHOLASTIC

Scholastic Children's Books,
Commonwealth House, 1–19 New Oxford Street,
London, WC1A 1NU, UK
A division of Scholastic Ltd
London ~ New York ~ Toronto ~ Sydney ~ Auckland
Mexico City ~ New Delhi ~ Hong Kong

First published in the UK by Scholastic Ltd, 2003

Copyright © Dean Wilkinson, 2003

ISBN 0 439 97836 X

Printed and bound by Nørhaven Paperback A/S, Denmark

10 9 8 7 6 5 4 3 2 1

The right of Dean Wilkinson to be identified
as the author of this work has been asserted by him in
accordance with the Copyright, Designs and Patents Act, 1988.

For my other daughter,
Alice Wilkinson

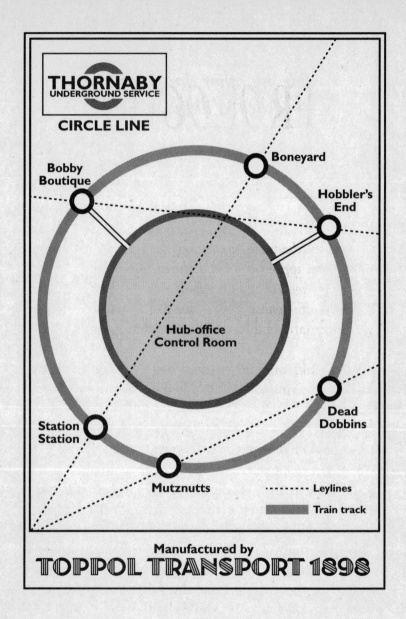

PROLOGUE

If you see the tracks vibrating,
The light approaching and ghosts all waiting,
Don't be worried in your bed,
'Tis only the ghost train – for you be dead.
    Thornaby children's rhyme from around 1900

Some old nursery rhymes have a basis in fact. "Ring a ring o' Roses" is based on the bubonic plague.

A-tishoo a-tishoo we all fall down.

That refers to the symptoms of the plague and the eventual falling down is the agonizing death. Which is nice for kiddies to sing about.

The Thornaby Ghost Train rhyme was a warning to kiddies to go to sleep and stay asleep all night. Otherwise they might hear the fabled Ghost Train which came for people who'd died in their sleep to take them off to the next world. If the people had been good, they got there straight away in first class, being served free tea and nice biscuits by resplendent angel trolley dollies. If they were bad people they had to sit in second class, in cramped smelly seats at the very back of the train so their journey took much longer.

It's interesting all our favourite nursery rhymes and fairy tales hark from times long gone. Perhaps in a few hundred years life and events of today will be remembered in such a way. Perhaps your descendants' kids will be singing. . .

There's A Shopping Trolley In The Beck!
(To the tune of "Three Blind Mice")
Oh flipping heck!
There's a shopping trolley in the beck.
It's just there next to the burnt-out Mazda.
It's rusted and bent and I think it's from Asda.
Oh flipping heck!
There's a shopping trolley in the beck.

Or telling fairy tales like . . . *Three Little Soap Stars Went To Town* (and disgraced themselves).

Or tongue twisters like . . . *Beckham Bounced And Booted His British Balls For Blighty.*

Perhaps.

So what has the old Thornaby Ghost Train rhyme have to do with anything today? What was it based on? Well, if you really want to know you're going to

2

have to read the whole book. So if you are reading this bit stood in some fancy bookshop, take it to the till and pay for it, damn you.

The Lord of Time's Prayer
as offered by The Cult of Temporal Renewal,
circa 1900

Our father time, who art in perpetual motion,
In decade and aeon be thy name,
Thy moments come, tick-tock be done,
In hours as it is in seconds.
Give us thy days 24 – 7 – 365,
Forgive not those who waste time unlike us,
And lead us not into bad time-keeping,
Deliver us from Newton,
Never ever is for ever,
Amen.

CHAPTER
ONE

The cat sat on the mat and wondered what the hell was going on. The black, middle-aged moggy usually had Sherwood Road to itself after midnight, even on a Thursday night – practically the beginning of the weekend. Apart from the occasional drunk, or taxi, or taxi full of drunks, or another cat from the really scruffy end of Thornaby looking for a fight, that is. Tonight was no exception. It was alone in the car port of number 55, but it sensed that things weren't right. There were strange vibrations coming from below the paths and road. The very ground seemed to resonate slightly and there was a low rumbling noise. The cat's hackles straightened, but it didn't know what it was frightened of. It walked out into the street and looked around. The rumbling died down and the cat felt braver. It slunk over to a gutter and peered down, seeing its own reflection gazing back up at it from the dirty water. It hissed at the wobbly moggy that lived down there which always responded at the exact same time. A few minutes later the vibration returned and then went again. The cat walked over to a metal manhole cover, sat on it and listened carefully.

Nothing.

Nothing at all.

Then suddenly something.

The cover burst off the manhole and shot up into the night air taking the cat with it. A huge blast of twinkling static electricity billowed out of the hole and arced across the street, instantly clinging to the metal doorhandle of the nearest house. The electricity flickered and vanished, leaving what can only be described as a Rip, or tear, in the night air showing multi-coloured flashes inside it. The baffling enigma hung in the air until a breeze gently wafted it closer towards the house.

* * *

Melvyn Havilland didn't live in a house any more. Since the 67 year old's young girlfriend moved in (Lynn was 61) his lonely old council house in Sherwood Road had magically transformed into a home. She'd turned his lonely world upside down and he was eternally grateful for that. Apart from filling a big hole in his life, he was seeing things he'd never seen before, or hadn't for some time. She cooked him three square meals a day and he saw what proper nutrition meant. (That it wasn't making sure you changed the flavours of the three Pot Noodles you had in any 24 hours.) When she hoovered up Mel saw a need for pride in one's surroundings, not to mention the pattern on the carpet he hadn't seen in ten years. And when she cleaned his windows Mel saw the garden he'd forgotten about too.

More importantly he saw that no matter your age, you're never too old to fall in love.

He was in his kitchen slapping a radio clock that had gone silly. He had put the kettle on the gas and lit a match when he noticed the digits on the clock display flickering and changing rapidly, going first forward, then back, then forward again.

"Useless piece of junk," he said as he dropped it back on to the kitchen sideboard. He checked his wristwatch and it too was being daft, the hands whirring first forward then back. He slapped the face and gave up trying to find out the exact time. Besides, he knew it was just after midnight because that's when the ten minute Naughty TV free-view ended on cable.

The kettle was boiling so he turned off the gas and reached for two mugs. He smiled, as he always did when making late night cocoa, because he no longer needed one cup, he was a two-cup guy now. Glancing outside into the inky black night he thought he saw what looked like a cat land on his front lawn and scamper away. Then a metal manhole cover landed in the grass with a *shump* noise as it stopped dead, half embedded in the lawn. Mel blinked his eyes and decided he was more tired than he realized.

Then it happened.

His body jolted and froze. He dropped the cups, but they didn't immediately smash on the floor. They stopped dead and just hung in the air. Everything seemed to suddenly stop, even the sound of the kettle's gentle bubbling. Mel's eyes seemed to slam shut for a moment and . . . then it was over.

Smash went the cups.

He steadied himself on the fridge and wondered what was happening to him.

A stroke?

Heart attack?

No, just a dizzy spell and it was quickly subsiding. All he felt now was a tad breathless and light-headed.

"Morning, lover," said Lynn, entering the kitchen drying her hair with a towel. Mel swung round to see her and yelled. She pulled a puzzled face. "I never heard you come to bed last night. Or get up for that matter." Then she noticed the smashed crockery and the look of sheer panic on Mel's face.

He was trying to take in what she had said. He glanced out of the window and where, only seconds ago, he'd seen the dark, orange streetlamp-lit road, he saw a bright sunlit early morning view. He touched the kettle and it was stone cold. He looked at his watch: it now said 7:37.

Mel Havilland had just lost over seven hours of his life and he hadn't the faintest idea of how it had happened. He felt a fresh wave of panic wash over him and he ran upstairs to his bedroom and sought out a cardboard box at the back of the wardrobe. He ripped open the lid and took out what was inside and gulped. It was a cat's head atop a rusty spike mounted on an old wooden board. The thing was long dead, half mummified, half decayed and its eyes were sewn shut. As keeper of The Grinning Cat's Head, Mel had seen this grizzly thing a million times, but even he was alarmed to see this barometer of evil smiling so widely. He knew that the bigger the grin the bigger the misfortune coming to the area. And he had never in his many years seen such a happy-looking thing of evil.

* * *

Gwen Lott reached over and slapped the snooze button on her alarm clock for the fourth time. 7:40 a.m., it read. She knew she couldn't allow herself another ten minutes' snooze as she had to get ready for school. She got up, yawned, and stepped over to the window. She pulled back the curtains and instantly woke up fully with a scream. For outside her window was Arthur King, his nose pressed against the glass and smiling idiotically.

"Good morning, Gwen. Hope I didn't startle you," he said nicely. "I just wanted to show you something."

"Arthur! What are you doing outside my bedroom window?" she bellowed.

Then she suddenly realized something else. "My upstairs bedroom window!"

"That's what I wanted to show you, Gwen. My new stilts."

Gwen pushed open the window and leant out. Arthur was indeed on stilts and very wobbly on them he was too. He clung tightly on to the brick-work of the house.

"Stilts!" cried Gwen.

Lawrence, Gwen's younger brother, poked his head out of the next window along and yawned.

"Hi, Arthur. Gosh, are you still there?" he said, wiping sleep out of his eyes.

Arthur nodded and smiled.

"What do you mean 'Still there', Lawrence? What time did this nonsense begin?"

"Nine o'clock last night. He climbed up on them to surprise you and kind of got stuck."

Arthur nodded nicely to Gwen.

"You've been outside my bedroom window all night?" gasped Gwen.

"Yes. Yes I have. Initially I was just going to surprise you. Then I lost my balance and had to hang on to the house. Then I was going to ask you to let me in, but I thought, no, she'll think I'm a wimp. Then I thought, yes, ask for Gwen's help. Then I thought, no, she'll think I'm a wimp. Then I thought yes, ask for Gwen's help. Then I—"

"Arthur!" snapped Gwen angrily.

"Well to cut a very very long story short, it went on like that for a while. All night. Until now when you opened the curtains. Please can I come in as I'm going to be late for school otherwise. Plus I need another wee."

"*Another* wee?" she asked as she peered further out and saw the long dark stain down the wall.

Arthur cringed with embarrassment.

"It won't dry." He cringed more. "It gets worse."

"How worse?" asked Gwen tentatively.

"Just don't look in your dad's rose bushes."

* * *

An hour later Gwen, Lawrence and a cleaned-up, fed and watered Arthur were walking along Trenchard Avenue for school. Gwen had wondered what Arthur's parents would say when he explained where he'd been all night, but they were cool about it, mainly because things like that tended to happen to Arthur quite a lot. It was just one of those things. In the thirteen years he'd been their son, Mr and Mrs King had come to accept that their only child was, for want of a better word, odd. They loved him dearly, and always would; it was just that Arthur never did anything that you'd expect a kid to do. One of the first instances of oddness was when he was a toddler. He went missing in Debenhams in Stockton. They found him staring unblinkingly at a showroom dummy as he was positive if he looked long enough at it it would move.* As he got older he became more eccentric, like when he was five he

---

* He still did this, actually. From time to time.

called the police about a murder he'd committed. They came round too, and found the body of a snowman he'd lain to rest in the freezer. Apparently he was sure it moved of its own accord and had wrestled it to the ground to prevent it escaping. When it broke apart he'd felt overwhelming guilt and called the rozzers to come and arrest him.

Other things he'd done were. . .

Filled his bedroom with sand and wrapped everything in silver paper so he could see what it was like to live on an alien planet.

Convinced himself he could speak "dog" and fallen out with a neighbour's collie over a debate about *Star Trek*. (Actually it had just bitten him.)

And once chased a butterfly so far that he needed to get a train home.

As a consequence Arthur never really had any friends (except the collie when they made up) and viewed anyone outside his own weird world with suspicion and distrust. But now he had a friend, Lawrence, who seemed to have just settled in to Arthur's world, despite being only 11 and seemingly quite sane. And Gwen, who was 15 and really shouldn't be talking to a third year, but liked Arthur really. Deep down. Way deep down.

Gwen noticed how very much Arthur was like his dad. Tall, thin, with a scruffy bush of dark brown hair and an ever present look of puzzlement on his face. Apart from when Arthur was leering lustily at her. She could see him doing it again out of the corner of her eye at the moment, but each time she turned to scowl at him he had already turned away and adopted his usual facial expression. After a few minutes of trying to catch him out Gwen gave up.

Lawrence was lagging behind stomping on loose paving slabs and listening hard. He intermittently stopped to look down the bigger cracks in the pavement, or ruptures in tarmac on the road. Altogether this was weird behaviour too, but Gwen was getting quite used to it as Lawrence had grown ever more eccentric since he'd hooked up with that loony Arthur King. Still, she should be grateful for small mercies. At least they no longer thought of themselves as the living reincarnations of King Arthur and Sir Lancelot. Crikey, what a palaver that caused.

They had a habit of aspiring to be great Britons, living and fictional, like Robin Hood and Little John, or Winston Churchill and Lord Mountbatten. Their bizarre role-playing always managed to get them into trouble, taking the ever suffering Gwen with them. Thankfully they had been themselves for some weeks now and the weirdness was at an all-time low.

Gwen checked all her blouse buttons were done up, for the fiftieth time, and said, "Arthur, if you don't stop looking at me like that I am going to kick your head in."

She turned to look at him but again he was too quick. He had stopped a few steps behind her and was already peering down a gutter with Lawrence.

"I definitely heard something last night. I did," said Lawrence. "It woke me up."

"Hmmm, me too. I couldn't get back to sleep for ages," replied Arthur.

Gwen wondered how Arthur had managed to sleep at all five metres in the air clinging on to a house, but didn't bother to ask.

"Don't say you're both going on about that stupid Ghost Train legend again. You think it's true?" sighed Gwen as she turned back and stood over them.

"Do checkout girls have love bites?" said Lawrence. "Of course it's true."

Arthur gazed up at Gwen, the woman he loved, and saw her face in partial silhouette against the bright morning sun. Oh she was a vision of loveliness, he mused. Beautiful . . . with long blonde hair, blue eyes and full lips. The kind of woman you cherish and respect. The kind of woman you'd die for. Plus, he could see straight through her skirt and make out the outline of her thighs.

"There's definitely something in it at least, thighs— er, I mean Gwen," said Arthur. "All legends have some basis in fact. I'll bet you someone, somewhere died last night."

"Well of course someone died. People are dying all the time. It doesn't mean a Ghost Train came to take their spirits away. The noises people have been hearing are just old waterworks, or pipes or something," she said.

Arthur and Lawrence gave each other a *"Yeah, right"* look and got up.

The three walked on.

"Anyway," carried on Gwen after a bit, "Mr Toppol says the Ghost Train is now a modern folk tale."

Arthur grimaced at the sound of Mr Toppol's loathsome name. Mr Toppol was the handsome, witty young physics teacher *all* the girls had developed crushes on since he'd started to teach at Bassleton Secondary School a few months ago. Gwen especially had a thing for him, which made Arthur's blood boil. Arthur had vowed to himself to start working out so he could get all big and muscly, then give Mr Toppol a smack in the mouth. But he still hadn't got round to it.

"You know – an urban myth," continued Gwen. "Like the dog who ate the TV remote control and walks round Thornaby changing people's TV channels every time it barks."

"Or the bus driver who was once nice to a kid. I heard that one was definitely true," said Lawrence.

"Rubbish," said Gwen. "They're all just nonsense tales."

"Well that just goes to show what an ill-educated dipstick Mr Toppol really is. Pah. Calls himself a teacher," snapped Arthur, shaking his head. "All he should call himself is a taxi and take it out of town. No one likes him. Not really. He's a complete twerp. And I hear he drinks. Oh yeah, it's true. And the girls are wasting their time fancying him because he lives with another man, I bet."

Luckily, no one heard the slanderous, bitter lies Arthur was spouting because Gwen had walked on and Lawrence was ten metres away with his head down a hole the council had dug six months ago for no apparent reason whatsoever. By the time the three had reached school Gwen had spoken non-stop about Mr Toppol and some of the funny things he had said, scarcely taking time to draw breath.

Arthur interrupted her. "I reckon the Ghost Train is more than an urban myth and it warrants further investigation."

"Really? Shall we do it then?" asked Lawrence, his face lighting up.

"Yeah. I reckon so. I was giving it some deep thought whilst Gwen was droning on about Mr Toppol." Arthur gave Gwen a sneer and she returned it, setting off for her form class.

"Fine," she shouted back at them, "Go on and waste your time playing detectives. Who do you think you are, Sherlock Holmes and Dr Watson? Ha!"

Gwen stopped dead in her tracks, suddenly realizing the dangerous seed she had just planted in the fanciful pair's heads. She swung round and her heart sank further when she saw the glazed look in their eyes and the broadening smiles forming on their faces.

"Yes! That's it. That's who we are, Lawrence. It's our next mission!" gasped Arthur. "I am Sherlock Holmes!

I see that now. In fact I have always known it! Well, I've always thought I'd look good with a pipe at least!"

"I so agree with you, Holmes. And I am Watson. I am Dr John Watson!"

"Oh bloody hell," said Gwen, and walked off wondering what stupid and ridiculous trouble she'd brought upon herself this time.

Arthur and Lawrence's minds were spinning with ideas and possibilities.

"If I am Sherlock Holmes I am going to need a whole new wardrobe," said Arthur.

"You mean a deerstalker hat and a tweed coat and that?"

"No, I mean a new wardrobe. To sit in. Don't you ever sit in your wardrobe to think about things?" asked Arthur.

"Frankly, no. But I have yet to achieve your level of mental turmoil, Arthur."

The boys thought hard about how this new dynamic would work for them. Lawrence clicked his fingers.

"The Ghost Train legend is from the era that Holmes first appeared in the *Strand Magazine*. It's fate that we should realize who we are meant to be just as the Ghost Train returns. Arthur, we have a mystery to solve."

"Yes, and as soon as I prove that Mr Toppol is a pervert, unfit to teach in this school, we shall solve that mystery. Hmm, I shall put him under surveillance."

"No, Arthur, Mr Toppol doesn't enter into this. It's the Ghost Train that's the mystery."

"Then he's something to do with that very mystery and I shall not rest until I implicate him in the dire plot. Whatever that dire plot is, of course. Until the striking of the lunch-bell, Watson," said Arthur in his best upper-class English accent, striding proudly into school.

"Arthur, wait. Your vendetta against Mr Toppol, albeit a worthy cause, will prove to be a distraction from our Ghost Train case. Forget him."

"Nonsense. The two are inexorably linked. It's quite elementary, my dear Lawrence. The game's afoot, old boy!" And with that Arthur disappeared into the crowd of his bustling, nudging fellow pupils whom he now considered to be akin to the filthy, disease-ridden – yet chirpy – cockney waifs who abounded in the streets of London over a hundred years ago.

CHAPTER
TWO

A cross town, on the banks of the multi-coloured River Tees, in a rickety allotment shed made out of old doors, old tables and other old allotment sheds, Walter Hill sat down to read the *Sport*. He'd just spent the last hour planting some lettuce, carrot and cauliflower seeds in neat rows along his two-metre allotment, and was taking a well-earned tea break.

"*Miracle Grow*," the packet read. "*If these seeds grow, it's a Miracle.*"

Walter loved his vegetables. He thought of nothing but vegetables. He spent all morning nurturing his vegetable plot and all afternoon in the Oddfellows Arms talking about them to his allotment chums, all of whom shared his interest in vegetables. He poured a mug of strong tea from his flask and surveyed the pages of the tawdry newspaper.

He said, "You don't get many of those to the pound," and for once he wasn't talking about vegetables.

Then he suddenly felt an altogether eerie sensation. He noticed at once the birdsong outside had stopped. So had the noise of the traffic from Thornaby Road. The air became very intense, charged with static, and he could taste tin in his mouth: ozone. He felt dizzy and stumbled off his stool and outside for some air. He was shocked to see a large twinkling oval shape surrounding the centre of his allotment. It looked as if the very air had somehow split. Within the Rip he saw hazy shapes behind an opaque curtain of sparkling stars. The whole thing pulsated, making a low buzzing sound like an electric motor.

And then it was gone.

Vanished.

Instantly the sound of birds and traffic began again, but this wasn't why old Walter fell flat on his backside, eyes bulging, too frightened to breathe.

Oh no.

He was terrified at the sight of an oak tree in the middle of his allotment patch which definitely wasn't there a moment ago. He would have noticed something like that as the tree was, judging by its size, a few hundred years old. He wasn't to know it, but it was an oak tree snatched from the future. An oak tree that shouldn't have been there for at least another five centuries. Walter ran into the shed and snatched up the empty seed packet. Miracle Grow. "Well I'll be a monkey's uncle. They're gonna make a flaming fortune!" he gasped to himself.

Similar disturbances in the flow of time were occurring in the boys' toilets at Bassleton School. Lawrence was alone in there after delivering messages from his maths tutor to several other teachers telling them which pub they'd all be meeting in for liquid-lunchtime.

He had delivered the notes in good time and decided to spend a penny in peace before the mad dinner-hour yellow-river-flood.* He had just shaken and zipped and was wiping his hands on his blazer when he became aware that the familiar sound of the broken toilet in trap number three had suddenly stopped. This was weird because ever since the school had been built in the 1960s that toilet had been faulty. It was some old law that in every public convenience one toilet had to be faulty at *all* times. His head started to swim and he suddenly felt sick. He staggered and supported himself on the nearest sink. He gasped as the very air inside the third cubicle rippled and twinkled. It literally split open and from inside the Rip, hovering centimetres above the ground, two apelike faces peered out. The hairy mugs were atop two squat hairy bodies and the two Neanderthal types were very intrigued by Lawrence. He could neither yell nor breathe for sheer fright. The Neanderthals suddenly leapt out of the Rip and landed on the tiled toilet floor. Instantly they were

* *Boys are terrible at aiming and this gets worse with age, trust me – Author.*

on him. One held his arms while the other tore at his clothes with frenzied curiosity. Lawrence tried to struggle, but the first Neanderthal held him tighter. The second pulled the pencil case from his inside pocket and all the coins from his trousers. It then foraged around his clothes and person until it had his Bic pen, his watch and his school tie. Then they let him drop to the floor and bounded back into the Time Rip. Lawrence could have sworn he saw them chuckle as the Rip closed up and vanished. Then the sound of the broken toilet returned and Lawrence was left breathless and bruised on the floor. He looked at his torn and tattered clothes. "Oh great. Mum's never going to believe this one."

* * *

The last of the pupils filed out of the physics room after collecting their coats from the rack. Each of them sighed and silently gestured at the boy-shaped lump in the last remaining inside-out coat, and the long legs sticking out from under it.

The room was a typical school science room. It had that ungodly sulphurous smell you just knew Hell smelt like. On the walls were yellowed and graffiti-ruined posters showing scientific information nobody would ever really need in life.* Periodic

---

* Like algebra and long division, you will NEVER EVER need these things in adult life so you must flatly refuse to do them. It's your duty.

tables and the chemical symbols for things like gold, bronze, cheese and dolphins etc. The benches were all stained and burnt and had kids' names for ever etched into them in acid and spent match heads. The teacher, Mr Toppol, sat at his desk and took off his glasses. He looked at the boy-shaped lump and wondered what to do. Lesta Toppol was a strong-jawed, handsome, slender man with collar-length fair hair swept back. He wore the regimental science teacher's uniform. The corduroy jacket with leather patches on the arms, the checked short-sleeved shirt, and always seemed to have the longest bit of his brown tie slung back over his shoulder. Since joining the Bassleton teaching staff he had risen quickly to being the most popular teacher in school. Mind you, that's not so difficult when all the competition is fat ugly maths teachers and French tutors whose dress sense harks back to the 1967 Paris Fashion Show.

Mr Toppol chewed his little fingernail and wondered how best to address the semi-concealed boy who had been hiding in his class throughout the previous lesson. He'd noticed him straight away, as had everyone, but was far too polite to make a spectacle of the boy in front of an entire class.

But now they'd gone for lunch.

"Erm," Mr Toppol said, then coughed. "Arthur, would you like me to go and get you a sandwich, or will you be leaving the coat rack to take lunch with the other pupils in the hall?"

Arthur slowly moved his own coat to one side and eyed Mr Toppol curiously. "How did you know I was here?" asked the boy King.

"I saw you come in, hang your coat up and hide behind it. Curious behaviour enough, some might say, but you stuck out because I know you're not a member of 2PMY."

"That doesn't explain how you know my name's Arthur."

"I have heard talk of you. Oh, and I read the large tag showing on the inside of your coat."

Arthur shifted his eyes to see the massive sewn-in name-tag with PROPERTY OF ARTHUR KING written on it. He cursed his mother for her lack of faith in him. "But you have to admire my panther-like agility to stay stock-still for the entire hour," he said.

"I do, I'm very impressed. You must have muscles and sinew like iron. Well done. No, it was the humming you were doing that wasn't so impressive."

"Oh right. Yeah well, you know what it's like when you have a song stuck in your head."

"I know, I know, I do, I truly do. Erm, it's the one off that sanitary towel advert isn't it? You sang it well."

"I was singing too?" asked Arthur incredulously.

"Yes. And snoring. You must have nodded off."

"Oh right. I had a bit of a rough night," sighed Arthur, stepping out from behind his coat. He looked Mr Toppol up and down and shook his head, totally unimpressed by this handsome and sweet-natured individual. Good-looking and kind, what right-minded woman would be taken in by so little? thought Arthur. Mr Toppol smiled nicely and a pregnant pause gave birth to an awkward moment.

"Why are you spying on me, Arthur?" asked Mr Toppol finally. "Have I done something to offend you? I apologize if I have."

"Spying on you! Don't flatter yourself."

"Is it extra science, then? If you want you can join my after-school science club. I do one every Monday, Wednesday and Friday night. They're very popular, but I could squeeze you in tonight if you like. Shall I pencil you in?" Mr Toppol took a slip of paper from his desk and signed it. He offered it to Arthur. "It's an after-school pass. You'll need it to stay on school property. All my club members need one." He smiled and nodded at the slip of paper.

"Don't try and get round me, I don't want free membership to your fan club, thank you very much, Toppol."

"It's fun. We aren't governed by the national curriculum so we learn entertaining science things. How to make things blow up or disappear, cool stuff like you see on *How 2*. I made a pupil glow in the dark last week. It was a right laugh."

"It sounds awful. I wouldn't be seen dead at some poxy after-school science club," sneered Arthur.

"Gwen Lott's coming tonight," said Mr Toppol, smiling knowingly.

Arthur snatched the pass and quickly stuffed it in his pocket. "Fine, I'll come to your science club, Herr Toppol, but I'll be dammed if I'll enjoy myself." Arthur began to stride out.

"See you tonight, Arthur. Oh and don't call me Toppol tonight."

"Oh I get it, master and servant, eh? Yes, *Mr* Toppol. No, *Mr* Toppol. So you're not the easygoing guy they claim after all. I knew you'd show your true colours sooner or later."

"No, I mean you can call me by my first name."

"Oh, right," said Arthur, making a fist in his pocket.

"It's Lesta. That's not Lester, it's spelt like a Teessider would say it, L – E – S – T – A. Lesta. My family go back hundreds of years on Teesside and have always been proud of our Teesside accent. You know how outsiders would say Redcar, have you noticed we say *Redca'*, missing off the last r? Or *Frida'* instead of Friday. Well, it's a tribute to that. But hey, I don't suppose you want to hear a boring old story about northern colloquialisms and my family history, do you."

And Mr Toppol was quite correct, Arthur did not, for he had left the room a good ten seconds ago.

CHAPTER THREE

Ms Brasscastle held Shakespeare's *Much Ado about Nothing** * in her hand and pulled a puzzled face. Like all female librarians, she was as ugly as sin, so coupled with a look of perplexity she resembled a horse that had just eaten a dung-dipped carrot by mistake. She couldn't understand how the kids had done it. There'd only been two people in the library all morning. The first being Abnormal Norman, and all he had done was read the exact same motorbike manual he had done every day for eight years (despite never once owning a motorbike). The other was the odd little boy who came in every day to ogle her. Lawrence, she thought his name was. Or something. And he came in after the event. So how had someone got in, written graffiti in the Shakespeare book and thrown it at her?

It had all happened like this.

She was holding the book, about to replace it to

* Actually it wasn't Shakespeare's, it was Stockton Borough Council's.

its proper shelf, whilst eagerly watching the time on the computer clock. She loved this part of the day. Library rules stated that books had to be back by midday on the date stamp otherwise a fine would be incurred. Today, when the clock reached twelve she could officially fine three different people 10p each who had outstanding books on loan. This was an exciting moment for her as her life was emptier than a rock star's moral bag.

All of a sudden everything had gone quiet, as though time had stopped. The computer clock flicked to random times. She felt dizzy and sick and must have passed out. The last thing she saw was what seemed like a fissure opening in the very air in front of her. In the Rip she honestly thought she saw a bald-headed man, with a beard, wearing very old-fashioned clothes, sitting at a desk and looking at her. She panicked and threw the book at him. She had tried to turn and run but her legs buckled with the nausea and she fell to the floor. Next thing, the book came flying out of the Rip, clocked her on the back of the head and she'd blacked out.

Now she was awake, the Rip had gone, every sound was as it should be, but the book had been written in. She read the inscription again. . .

Look wench, I know not what trickery this be, but if thou art so desirous for an autograph, next time seeketh out mine agent!

Bill Shakespeare

Obviously this was a sick trick. She reached out a long and creepy finger and touched the writing. It was still wet.

* * *

Lawrence was in the small, sectioned-off reference room of Thornaby Library. He spent a lot of free time there as he had access to all the books nobody else wanted to read. Plus he could occasionally ogle the delicious Ms Brasscastle, the woman he wanted to marry*, through the glass.

Lawrence turned over another page in another old and faded book from the large pile he'd taken from the dusty shelves. This book, more a pamphlet, was dated April 1900 and entitled *What's on in Thornaby*. It featured some exciting up-and-coming events of the era and had small news headlines such as. . .

Tri-County Pig-Kicking Finals Postponed!
Loud Woman To Be Sent To Asylum
and
Thornaby Green Witchcraft Ducks Escape Retribution By Flying Away

Lawrence re-read a small paragraph which read—
  "Thornaby Underground To Be Filled In," said

---

* *This is because she was the only woman he had ever seen totally nude. See* The Legend of Arthur King *for the distressing details.*

29

Arthur looking over Lawrence's shoulder and making the already jumpy youth launch out of his seat and spin round with his fists drawn. Arthur had walked in a minute ago, but Lawrence hadn't noticed.

"Arthur, you idiot! You frightened the breakfast out of me! Don't do that!" he yelled. He took a deep breath. "I thought you were those monkey men again. Ooh, I like your hat, where did you get it?"

"I had an idea Mel might have one," said Arthur, proudly taking off the deerstalker cap and spinning it in his fingers. He pulled a large, floppy, tweed fishing hat from his pocket and put it on Lawrence's head. "This is the closest he had to a Dr Watson hat. Not that there is such a thing, but Mel swears Nigel Bruce wore one in the old Basil Rathbone Sherlock Holmes films. Do you like it?"

"Do post offices reek of sweat?" said Lawrence gleefully. "Of course I do. It's brilliant. Thanks." He pulled the hat further on to his head.

"He's having a look for a pipe for me. And a magnifying glass," said Arthur. His face turned serious. "So what's all this then? I thought you were going to help me get some dirt on Mr Toppol the pick-pocketing, alcoholic kitten-drowner. Do you know, Mr Toppol lets pupils use his first name."

"That *has* to be a sackable offence, Arthur," said Lawrence, shaking his head in disgust.

"You'd have thought so, but our glorious deputy

head Mr Bedivere said it wasn't when I reported it to him not ten minutes ago."

Arthur looked at the books his young friend had been reading. "Toppol claims his family has been around these parts for donkey's years. Have you uncovered any history of insanity that might get him sacked?"

"Arthur, you know I explained earlier that Mr Toppol's got absolutely nothing to do with the Ghost Train mystery."

Arthur sighed and sat down.

"Yes, I suppose I was letting my hatred for the oily creep get in the way of our case. I'll forget all about him from now on."

"No! He has got something to do with it. Or his family has!"

"I knew he was up to something!" said Arthur gleefully. "Say on."

"Well, amazingly I've found out there's a history of eccentricity in his family."

"*Ergo* he's mentally unstable, *ergo* he's not fit to teach," said Arthur smiling widely.

Lawrence nodded, happy his best chum was happy with his findings.*

"Say on, Watson, say on," said Arthur excitedly.

"His great-great-grandfather was a scientist and inventor called Elle Toppol, and apparently he was a

---

* The irony didn't occur to these two that their misguided belief they were Sherlock Holmes and Watson was incredibly eccentric. But irony was always lost on them.

freaky ga-ga-chumper. You know, bonkers. But, he was incredibly wealthy so they couldn't cart him off to the funny farm. In 1896, he commissioned the Thornaby Underground. A train system with one Circle Line here in Thornaby. Obviously it was all on a much smaller scale than the London Underground."

"A *much* smaller scale. I mean, how stupid, an underground train service in Thornaby? The town's only eight kilometres across. What possible use could that be?" laughed Arthur scornfully. "Typical of *his* family. Full of their own self-importance."

"It would seem so, Arthur. It closed just after it was completed in 1900 and apparently was filled in. All stations were torn down and the land sold. Toppol's Folly they called it. Here's a map of it."

Arthur surveyed the yellowed tube map printed in the aged pamphlet. In faded pink-red ink was a circle with six black dots signifying the stations. Next to this was a crude, hand-drawn map of Thornaby, also with the stations marked on. He vaguely recognized it to be his home town because so much had obviously changed in a century.

"If it really was true, it must have been a massive undertaking and took four years to complete. And then, just filled in again."

"Well done, Lawrence. This proves Toppol's of insane stock. Now all we have to do is take this evidence to the deputy head and demand he be fired forthwith. Come on, Watson, the game's afoot again."

Lawrence pulled Arthur's blazer to stop him leaving.

"Arthur, you're missing the bigger picture. What if the Thornaby Underground wasn't filled in after all? What if that was just part of the story? What if Elle Toppol wanted people to believe it was gone? He could have easily done it, what with all his money. Rich men can do anything these days and, crikey, a century ago the rich were almost god-like. Maybe the sounds of the Ghost Train are in fact the Underground from a hundred years ago. Look!"

Lawrence wrenched open a book only he and Arthur had ever bothered reading in the thirty-odd years it had lain in the reference library. It was called *Myths and Legends of Thornaby*, but whoever had written it was a mystery as the name had long since faded. He found the page on the Ghost Train. He pointed to a date in the text. "It says here the Ghost Train noises stopped around 1908. Look at the date when Elle Toppol died," he said, pointing to another open old book entitled *Influential People and Exciting Killers from Teesside*. "It's the same year, 1908."

Arthur sat down and perused the books. He chewed his thumb like the mouthpiece of a pipe. "I'm getting confused, old boy – where's this leading?"

"I don't know, Arthur. All I can tell you is that it's just possible that someone has uncovered the long-abandoned Underground railway track and is running a train along it late at night. Why? I haven't a clue."

They stopped and thought for a second, but no reasons sprang to mind.

Lawrence checked his watch to see how much of the dinner hour was left. It was gone and he remembered the cavemen who had mugged him earlier. He shuddered and thought for a second.

"Arthur, have you heard about these Time Rips people have being going on about? This phenomena where things and people are being affected by a tear in the very fabric of time itself?"

"Vaguely. It's interesting, but it's hardly credible. It's like alien abduction – how come these Time Rips only happen to oddballs? It happened to Mel last night. I mean, he's great and all that, but he's a bit senile, isn't he?"

"I'm not and it's just happened to me."

"What?"

"It's happening all around Thornaby," said Lawrence. He pulled a copy of *Fortean Times* out of his Asda/school bag and flicked through it. He jabbed at a page. "There!"

Arthur looked at the article in the journal of unexplained phenomena. A small paragraph read. . .

"TIME GENTLEMEN, PLEASE."
The North East town of Thornaby has been hit by another alleged Time Rip. After FT *reported this phenomena last ish, snippets have been sent to us*

from the Evening Gazette *(some local paper or other), regarding people losing hours and days of time. Now it would seem the outbreak of Time Rips (alleged ruptures in the fabric of time), are spreading. Harold Gimp, landlord of the Oddfellows Arms, claims a localized Rip appeared to him, and two men, neither of whom he had ever seen before, fell out of the tear beating the hell out of one other. They rolled around the floor, disrupting furniture, pummelling each other hard and fast until they fell back into the Rip, upon which it promptly closed. Two days later, the men came into his pub separately and after a few hours' hard drinking one noticed that the other one was looking at his pint in a disrespectful way. Fisticuffs broke out and the exact same tables and chairs were overturned in a carbon copy replay of the fight Mr Gimp had seen two days previously.*

As reports of Time Rips become more prevalent, it seems their effect is also heightening, with things being shifted spatially too. One Thornaby lady claims she saw the Great Sphinx of Egypt in her airing cupboard. This frightened her immensely on three counts.

1) In her vision, the Sphinx was under construction.

2) The work was overseen by scary alien life-forms with canine-like heads.

3) And, more importantly, someone reached

through the Rip and took all her best towels. "They were a wedding present!" said the lady, who has since turned to booze.

Arthur nodded slowly as well as sticking his bottom lip out, trying to make it look like he understood every word of the article, but was yet to deliver his thoughts on it.*

"I know these Time Rips are real, Arthur," said Lawrence. "I've seen one first hand. Something is causing time to temporarily split and glimpses into the past and future are coming through."

"Sinister. And Mel did say the Cat's Head is grinning again," said Arthur, puffing on his thumb. "I really must get a pipe."

"Two strange things. The Ghost Train and the Rips in time, and I wouldn't be at all surprised if they weren't connected. Two pieces in one big puzzle, I'll be bound."

"Plus we have the problem of getting Toppol sacked, so that makes three pieces to the puzzle," said Arthur, wagging his finger.

Lawrence sighed and smiled at his chum. "Yes, Arthur. Three pieces. But I fear more evidence must be gathered first. Come on," he said putting the books back on their shelves. "We'll be late for school."

"Indeed, old boy, the game's afoot," said Arthur,

* You do that too, don't you. Go on, admit it. You're probably doing it right now.

standing sharply. Under his breath he added, "Again."

They began walking out.

"Monkey men?" asked Arthur, pulling a face.

"I'll tell you on the way."

CHAPTER
FOUR

The school afternoon came and went with no real events to speak of. A first-year boy, who would soon know better, asked Arthur and Lawrence about their strange headwear and got the full Sherlock Holmes theory. He called them a couple of pillocks and walked off, realizing that in future they should be ignored at all costs.

"You, sir, have an odour," Arthur had shouted after him in his best upper-class English accent, but when the boy turned back round Arthur and Lawrence fled.

It was now home time. The massive schoolchild throng hurried off the grounds to the town centre to swear loudly in front of toddlers and harass the shopkeepers. Then home for tea and cable TV. A handful, however, of mixed-year kids (mainly girls) made their way to the physics lab for Mr Toppol's – sorry, *Lesta's* – after-school science club.

By the time Arthur and Lawrence set off for the club the lesson was well under way. Mr Toppol stood by the blackboard with his shirt sleeves rolled up and his tie off, trying to look as informal and streetwise as a teacher possibly can. Which is like asking a bear to mingle with chickens and not stand out.

Pinned to the board was a large blown-up photograph which he had covered with black paper, the black paper having several flaps cut in it. Mr Toppol surveyed the class who were silently reading a photocopied sheet of paper. Occasionally one of the girls (usually Gwen) would look up at sir and he'd reply with a lopsided smile and a wink. This made the girl (usually Gwen) go red, giggle and look back down. Any of the boys looking up would get one of Mr Toppol's manly thumbs-up and *Yup, I know where you're coming from, dude* looks.

The text they were reading began. . .

NOSTRILDAMUS
a brief study by Lesta Toppol

There was once a soothsayer in the dim and distant past whose revelations weren't quite on the scale of the legendary loudmouth show-off Nostradamus, but were staggeringly more accurate. And he didn't write his thoughts down in deliberately ambiguous four line quatrains to hedge his bets either.

Thornaby's Nostrildamus was a seer of the future and did so by reading his own dried snot and bogies. (Hence the nickname; his real name was Eric Chunderford.) And don't think reading one's own crusty mucus for visions of the future is so far-fetched. Voodoo priests read chicken entrails and gypsy fortune tellers read tea leaves. Other things people have seen the future in are:

The hairs on shower doors,

The vomit of drunken men,

And much more modernly the annoying shafts of sunlight you just cannot get off the TV screen when viewing it by day.

Here's an example of one of Nostrildamus's amazing predictions about his own town of Thornaby. . .

APE MEN OF THE FUTURE

By Chunderford, aka Nostrildamus, 1693 AD

In the years after two thousand, the second millennium, man will have evolved far from what we know today. He will have lost a large percentage of his intellect and live in small untidy box-like hovels. His clothes will be made of a shiny and garishly coloured material and his footwear elaborately streamlined for speed, but he will not make use of them.

Facial features will change also. There will no longer be hair covering his scalp, rendering the cranium metallic shiny.

His face will become like that of a snarling ape and a hairy mussel will replace the normal mouth and chin.

He will adorn his skin with war paint depicting tribal war cries and pictures.

He will pierce his own flesh with silver and gold, the more piercing the more fierce the warrior.

Gathering food and drink will be a pastime and he will have large fearsome hunting dogs to aid him in this pursuit. Once he has collected the food he will take it back to his tribe in specially constructed boxes.

His family will be of equal savagery and will be stirred into violent and aggressive stupors by frantic tribal drumming music with neither form nor creativity.

They will pray to their Gods by mental numbing, a state of near-hypnosis induced by sitting transfixed by a central point in their dwellings. This being a praying box to which their gods will appear. And any child daring to interrupt the religious ceremony will be smote most heartily and yelled at, with many profanities cursing said child's birth.

The female will also be strange by our appearances.

Her body weight will be tenfold and her posterior made large from the lengthy praying ritual.

She will wear ceremonial clothes such as very tight leggings to bloat her ankles. The more bloated the ankles, the louder the female. Indeed she will be equally as aggressive as the male.

Her hair will be unkempt and permanently wet.

The male children will mimic the elder males from an early age and exhibit the same ferocity and violent tongue. The female children will mimic the female elders and be eager to reproduce at their earliest chance so they too can exist in tiny box-like hovels and preach the religion of shouting and tribal drumming rites.

Nozza

"Anyone got any thoughts on this?" asked Mr Toppol, half-sitting on his desk. Nervously, Gwen put her hand up. "Well, it's wrong isn't it, sir – sorry, Lesta. Nostrildamus must have got his dates wrong. Maybe that's the kind of society that'll evolve in the thirty-first century, not the twenty-first."

"Top merits for observation to the beautiful girl at the front," said Mr Toppol clapping his hands.

Gwen felt ten feet tall. *He* thought *she* was beautiful. The other girls sneered at her.

Mr Toppol continued. "It does indeed sound like he was seeing far far into the future, but let's look at the facts." He stepped up to the blackboard and pulled down the first flap in the black paper. Behind it was the shiny, closely shaved cranium of a human being. Male.

"Observe, Nostrildamus said they would have shiny heads. Not unlike this one. And what of the tribal adornments of skin and piercings?' He pulled open two more flaps to show a bluebird drawn on to a large neck, and a ring through an earlobe. "The monkey's mussel." He pulled down a flap to reveal a set of lips surrounded by hair, very much like an ape's mouth (or a mussel). "The strange material of their clothes, garishly coloured." Again he pulled down a flap, this one showing a coat arm which had a bright purple and day-glo green pattern. "The hunting dogs." Another flap revealed a savage snarling dog's face. "Does anyone see a picture emerging here?" he asked.

Fay Morgan stuck up her hand and said, "It's some weird creature from a science fiction film, isn't it? And you're showing us bits of it. Am I right?'

He smiled and pointed at her. "No." He pulled away the entire black paper covering and everyone laughed in unison.

The picture showed a fat, shaven-headed and rough-looking man with a goatee beard, tattoos on his neck, and many piercings in his eyebrow, ears and nose. He was wearing a tracksuit, despite obviously never having done any sport judging by his portly figure. He had expensive, unmarked trainers on and he held a thick dog chain with a chunky, grievous-looking Rottweiler on the end of it, straining to get free and maul someone.

"Anyone recognize this alien creature? Of course, there's hundreds of him all over the place. Low intellect. Violent. Lazy. Probably sells drugs."

"What about the boxes, sir? Nostrildamus seems to think it's a culture fixated by boxes," asked Fay.

"Look at him, Fay. He obviously only eats take-away pizzas, which come in boxes, do they not? The hovel-like boxes are his council flat or home. And the box he prays to? TV. People like him sit for hours in near-hypnosis watching the dreaded television. And the wild tribal drumming sounds Nostrildamus heard? Well, you see a man like this and you can guarantee he'll have a vulgar car with a powerful stereo blasting out drum and bass or dance music. Anything that doesn't have an ounce of structure or melody to it."

"Nostrildamus is still wrong though, sir – sorry, Lesta," said Fay. "I mean, there may be a lot of louts like him around, and his horrible families, but not everyone's like that."

"Fine deduction, Fay. Top merits to you too. But put yourself in Nostrildamus's shoes. His used hanky only revealed a small section of society."

The class looked blank.

"Consider an alien explorer landing on Earth to discover how we live," Mr Toppol continued. "He may land in the Kalahari desert and see nothing but sand for hundreds of kilometres. He'd go back home and say, '*Earth is rubbish, it's nothing but a big beach and no sea.*' If he'd only touched down in Trafalgar Square he would have seen the wondrous sights of the capital city. The buildings. The cars. Living, breathing, sentient human beings. So perhaps Nostrildamus just saw this chap here and presumed this was what we were heading towards. So you were actually half right, Gwen."

She stuck her bottom lip out and nodded. He thought she was beautiful, she thought.

"Utter cobblers," said Arthur, who was now standing in the classroom with Lawrence behind him.

Mr Toppol jumped as he hadn't seen the fanciful two enter like the rest of the class had. "Arthur, you made it," he said.

Arthur took off his deerstalker cap. "No, I borrowed it, but thanks for noticing, Toppol," said the lad.

"Lesta, Arthur. My friends call me Lesta after school hours."

"I know, Toppol," said Arthur smugly.

"You look quite the sleuth, Arthur. A consulting detective worthy of reportage in the *Strand* itself."

"What?" said Arthur.

"Like Sherlock Holmes."

"Yes, I do."

There was an awkward pause broken by a knock at the classroom door.

"Don't come in just yet!" yelled Mr Toppol to the door. He turned to Arthur, his eyes alight with fun. "Here's your chance, Arthur. By that knock alone give me a description of the next person to enter this room." He turned to the class. "Sherlock Holmes could give a full description of someone from the tiniest shred of evidence."

"Very well," said Arthur confidently. "The person outside that door is tall. Hence the knock emanating from the upper part of the door. He is male, very young and has black hair. He has recently returned from a holiday of foreign climes where he gained a vulgar suntan to his face and neck. He is athletic, extremely thin and can speak no less than five different languages." Arthur looked at Mr Toppol smugly.

"Let us see," said the teacher. "Enter."

The class sniggered behind their hands when Fat Red Fred came in. He was the school caretaker. He was short with spiky ginger hair with the whitest, pastiest face you could imagine. He was extremely fat and unfit. He'd never left Teesside in his entire life and as for speaking five different languages, Fat Red Fred had barely mastered the basics of English.

"Dem two kids, like, am them in yer, like, class, like, or what, like, know what am mean, like?" mumbled the serious-looking caretaker.

"See," said Arthur grandly. "I told you he was male."

As Mr Toppol walked the caretaker out, explaining that Arthur and Lawrence were part of his science club, Lawrence wondered how Arthur could have been so amazingly wrong. Especially considering they knew Fat Red Fred was walking not ten metres behind them all the way through the deserted school corridors to the science block.

Arthur stepped up to the fifth-year boy sitting next to Gwen and whispered something in his ear. Mr Toppol stooped down to talk to Lawrence.

"And who might you be, son?"

"Son? If you're my dad then who's that bloke who sleeps in the same bed as my mum every night?"

Lawrence half smirked. The class and Mr Toppol burst into fits of laughter. Gwen didn't, she was beetroot-red with embarrassment as she always was when Lawrence and Arthur were in the same room as her – heck, the same ruddy town! She gave Lawrence a hard stare and mouthed the words, "You don't know me!"

He nodded to say he understood, then said, "I'm her brother," pointing at Gwen. She covered her eyes.

"Would you like to join the science club?" asked Mr Toppol. "We've always room for one more."

"Providing I don't have to sit near a lit Bunsen burner. I'm scared of naked flames," said Lawrence, going to find a seat.

"Oh my, why's that?" asked Mr Toppol gently.

"I have been ever since my dog caught fire."

"Your dog caught fire? How?"

"Dunno, one minute it was all right, the next it went *woof*," said Lawrence dryly.

Mr Toppol and the class roared with laughter again.

The fifth-year boy who Arthur had whispered to ran out of the class in sheer panic. Arthur had lied to him that he had seen a fire engine rushing to his house and suggested he get home quick to identify the bodies. Taking the space next to Gwen any thoughts of the reprisal slap the big boy would give him tomorrow were far from Arthur's mind. He smiled at Gwen. She sneered and checked all her blouse buttons were done up.

"Lawrence," said Mr Toppol, waving to the first-year. "Would you kindly return to the front of the class. And Fay, fetch the EMI device if you would."

The class collectively murmured and smiled. Mr Toppol grinned and put his finger to his lips. Fay trotted out to an adjoining room.

"What's an EMI device?" asked Lawrence, sensing he wasn't in on this particular joke.

"Oh nothing, you'll see," said Mr Toppol, patting him on the shoulder. "Arthur, while we wait for Miss Morgan to return, could you explain the thesis which culminated in your previous utterance regarding the seeings of Nostrildamus."

"Eh?"

"Why did you say 'cobblers'," hissed Gwen.

"Oh that. Well, you shouldn't judge people on their appearances, that's all. I mean, yes that baldy bloke does look like a wrong 'un, but what's to say he isn't the total opposite?"

"I don't follow, Arthur," said Mr Toppol, folding his arms and listening hard.

"You're looking at him as a stereotype rather than an individual. Granted he doesn't get many points out of ten for appearance, and if he does listen to dance music he's just unimaginative. He still might be a nice person. He must be a keen animal lover.

Look at that dog, its coat's shinier than his head. And while we're on the subject, how dare you speak ill of someone just because they live in a council property. I live in a council house and there's nothing wrong with me."

Gwen tutted and said, "Nothing a crack team of psychologists can't put right."

Mr Toppol looked at the picture again and craned his neck. "Arthur, you cloak me in shame," he said. "I have judged this man on appearance alone, and that is wrong."

"Who is it, sir?" asked Gwen, not liking how Arthur was one step ahead of Mr Toppol – sorry, Lesta – in the debate.

"Oh, I just took the image from *Crime Magazine*. He butchered some people who were trying to sell drugs on his patch." Mr Toppol remained looking at the picture. Gwen smirked at Arthur but the irony, as always, was lost on him and he was trying to imagine Gwen in a bikini.

Fay returned to the room with the electrical apparatus Mr Toppol had requested. The EMI (short for Electro-Magnetic Ineffectualator) was a small device screwed firmly to an oak base. In the centre was an orb-shaped glass and inside that was a filament with a tightly wrapped copper coil. Outside the orb were four brass-covered boxes which were some kind of battery, each one connected to the other, and to the orb. All around the oak board were small banks of circuits, coils, transistors, resistors, capacitors, diodes, wires, what-nots and God-knows. The whole thing looked very homemade, thought Arthur, and he reckoned more than half of the over-the-top electrical stuff did nothing and was only there to make Toppol look brainy.

"One hell of a Teasmade that, Mr Toppol," said Lawrence, closely examining it. Everyone laughed out loud again, especially Arthur who laughed much much longer than anyone else and only stopped when Gwen kicked him under the table.

"If only it were so useful, Lawrence. It's what I call an Electro-Magnetic Ineffectualator." He switched it on and the device whirred and hummed and suddenly a bright, dancing spark appeared inside the orb. It flitted and darted from the central coil, around the glass as if searching for a way out. "What do you think it does, Arthur?"

"Makes you look like you know something about science?" replied Arthur, yawning and crossing his arms. Mr Toppol smiled and chuckled, but the rest of the class didn't appreciate Arthur's lack of respect.

"Lawrence, pass me that sheet of paper please, and I'll show you what it does."

Lawrence leant forward to pick up the paper from the desk and the side of his head passed close to the orb. He yelped as his head felt like a piece of dirt being sucked in by a vacuum cleaner. The entire side of his face felt like it was being gently pulled off towards the machine. "Oi!" he yelled and jumped away from the device.

The boys in the class erupted into spontaneous laughter. The girls laughed too, but it was a half-hearted laugh mixed with much sympathetic girly "*aw*ing".

Lawrence rubbed his face and looked puzzled. "What was that?" he demanded.

More laughter. More "*aw*ing".

"Damn you, sir. Answer my colleague," Arthur shouted angrily over the class. "I warn you, Toppol, when my memoirs are published you shall be cast in the murkiest of lights."

"Arthur, it's fine, really," replied the teacher, laughing. Mr Toppol took Lawrence to one side and put his arm round him. "It's all right, Lawrence, I play that gag on all my new club members. Hey –" Mr Toppol whispered something into Lawrence's ear and he too smirked, now seeing the funny side.

"Yeah, good one. Hey, Arthur," said Lawrence, "come and look at this. It doesn't hurt."

Arthur shook his head and narrowed his eyes. "I'll not be your comedy monkey, Toppol," he said firmly, leaning back on his stool and falling off it. He quickly sat back up and regained his look of contempt. "What is that device?"

"It's what I said, an Electro-Magnetic Ineffectualator. It produces an electromagnetic field for no good reason. Hence the *ineffectual* bit. It doesn't do anything, it just looks good."

"Base the idea on yourself then?" said Arthur.

Gwen snapped. She roared, "Arthur, if you haven't got anything nice to say then don't say anything at all. Just naff off and play Poirot or Miss Marple or whatever it is you're pretending to be this week. You're a very sad and pathetic little boy. I really hate you sometimes, Arthur."

Stunned silence.

The sneer dropped from Arthur's face and he could feel himself going red. A pain in his chest grew then lowered to his stomach making him feel sick, like his heart had literally sunk. He took off his hat because he now felt very foolish and began to exit the room.

"Arthur, look, I'm sure we've just got off on the wrong foot," pleaded Mr Toppol as the boy left.

Arthur ignored the teacher. Lawrence looked down at the floor in the uneasy silence, then began to follow him out.

"Wait, Lawrence, here's some notes on the subjects we've covered already." Mr Toppol handed Lawrence a sealed A4-sized envelope. "It's all in there, space flight, telekinesis, I think you'd be particularly interested in my thoughts on urban myths and their relation to science."

Lawrence stuck out his bottom lip and nodded then went to catch Arthur up.

CHAPTER
FIVE

T he hypnotic silence that *Coronation Street* so richly deserves dissipated when the first couple of notes from the end theme began. Conversation was now allowed again. Arthur and Lawrence were sat in Mel and Lynn's living room drinking tea and eating biscuits. The elderly couple had been told about the science club and were on Arthur's side to the hilt.

"Sounds like a flash little creep to me," said Mel, picking up the conversation from exactly where it had ended when the commercial break did.

"You get oily little ticks like him, Arthur. All mouth and trousers," said Lynn patting Arthur's hand. Arthur smiled at the couple.

"A funny man, though," smiled Lawrence, who instantly became aware of Arthur's hard stare. "To laugh *at*, not with." He hastily stuffed another digestive in his mouth and looked back at the telly. "Ooh, Arthur. Here's that sanitary towel advert you love."

"She's totally besotted by this Mr Toppol,

though," said Arthur, deliberately ignoring Lawrence. "I've lost her. I think I've really lost her this time."

"Now now, Arthur, that's not true. You couldn't possibly lose Gwen," said Lynn, putting her arm round the despondent youth.

"She was never yours to begin with. She wouldn't touch you with a poo-dipped stick." This was Lawrence speaking again, but his un-thought-out remarks were hidden in the half-chewed biscuit.

"Arthur, things probably aren't as bad as they seem," Mel chipped in, and Lynn knew whatever the old goat was about to say probably wouldn't help matters a bit.

"It looks like a major motorway pile-up now, I'll admit. . ."

Lynn sighed.

"An overturned, jackknifed lorry and masses of mangled, wrecked cars all over the place," continued Mel. "But on closer inspection you'll find the cars were wrecked anyway and just fell off the lorry that was taking them to the scrapyard. No one's hurt. Even the driver of the lorry was flung to safety and landed on an old mattress."

Arthur raised his eyebrows. Oddly – or rather, not that oddly* – this made some sense to him. Lynn decided to stop Mel while he was ahead and change the subject.

* This is Arthur King we're talking about here.

"This Ghost Train thing is very interesting, you know. I did some research on it for that book I wrote. *Myths and Legends of Thornaby*."

The others didn't hear this as a trailer for *Who Wants To Be A Millionaire* was on and all attention was diverted to Chris Tarrant (and rightly so).

Lynn left the room to seek out her notes. The trailer finished.

"So Mel, lost any more time lately?" asked Lawrence.

"Not that I'm aware of. Mind you I did put my shoes in the oven today and the fishfingers in the shoe cupboard. Very eerie. Very *Twilight Zone*," said the old one.

"I think that's just stupidity, Mel. You've always been the same," mused Arthur.

"Happen you're right, Arthur. Best not bother *Fortean Times* with that one, Lawrence," said Mel.

Lynn returned with a collection of old yellowed maps and handwritten notes. She unfolded one of the maps and spread it neatly on the glass coffee table. It was an old ordnance survey map of Stockton and Thornaby-on-Tees, dated 1897. Arthur glanced at it and picked up another which he unfolded.

"Had these years, I have," said Lynn.

"Blimey, Lynn. How old are you?" asked Lawrence, pointing to the date.

"It's a reprint, dicky-der-brain," she laughed.

On the map was a red circle drawn on in pen. "The circle is the alleged route the Thornaby

Underground took. The six stations were at these points. Here, I've written down notes on them by the side."

STATION STATION
Unimaginatively named as this was the underground station directly under the overground mainline station.

MUTZNUTTS
Named after the Gentleman's Boarding Kennels owned by German-born D B Mutznutt & Son and situated next to this station's entrance. Mutznutts was a high class kennels and only the finest breeds of dog were allowed in.

DEAD DOBBINS
In relation to the glue factory above it.

HOBBLER'S END
Named after the false leg factory above ground.

BONEYARD
After Thornaby Cemetery above it.
NOTE: This station is at a slight dip. It had to be lower than the others so as not to upset the dignity of those at rest above the track. Besides, a rotten cadaver falling on the track might create more dead bodies.

BOBBY BOUTIQUE
Named after the police station which once stood above it.

"But the stations are long gone. They were bulldozed when the Circle Line was filled in. They all got built on, didn't they?" asked Lawrence.

"The overground entrances, yes. Wouldn't it be great if some pockets of these underground stations remained to this day, like your theory the track's still there too, Lawrence. It'd be fascinating to see it all."

Arthur was examining his map, also of Thornaby, but a much more modern one from the late 1960s. On the map someone had drawn on three black lines stretching off it at different angles, two of them crossing the other.

"What are these lines, Lynn? Roads or something? Overground train tracks?" asked Arthur, tracing the three lines with his finger. Lynn, Mel and Lawrence turned to examine the map Arthur held.

"Oh those, that's just some fanciful stuff I was investigating. They're alleged leylines. They're supposedly natural channels of Earth energy criss-crossing the planet. They have a power no one really understands. I just found all that living Earth hippy rubbish interesting in the sixties. But you don't want to hear about that, I'm sure, Arthur."

And she was right. He wasn't listening. Arthur had spotted something. He had put Mel's table-lamp under the glass coffee table so it shone through and placed the leyline map over the red circled map.

"If you look at the six points on that map where the stations are, then put this map with the leylines on top of it, what do you see?" he asked.

"A crack in the table I never saw before," said Mel.

"The maps, Mel. Let me align them first. There, how's that?"

There was a moment's silence as Arthur's findings were genuinely amazing. The six stations on the red circle map touched six different points on the leylines from the second map exactly.

"Each of the six stations is built on a leyline point. How odd," said Lawrence. "That is too much of a coincidence."

"Good Lord, Arthur. That's amazing! Well spotted," gasped Lynn. She shook her head. "You know, Arthur, sometimes I think you're the brightest person I have ever met. But at other times you're . . . well. . ."

"Well what?" asked Arthur with more than a hint of indignity.

"Other times you're one widdle short of a full lav," added Mel.

Arthur shrugged his shoulders and nodded.

Mel tapped the maps. "Admittedly it's a biggy, but it still *is* just a coincidence, isn't it?" asked the aged one.

"Maybe not. There's natural power in leylines, Mel. The Earth's very own EM field, electro-magnetic energy," Lynn pointed out.

"And who do we know who likes showing off his electrical expertise?" asked Arthur, nodding at Lawrence.

Lawrence nodded knowingly back then said, "I dunno. Who?"

"Toppol."

"Yes. Yes of course!" said Lawrence suddenly.

"If you could create a circuit which touched on each of the six points on the leylines, you could, if you were clever enough, release the natural energy. Rather like hitting two pieces of flint together to create a spark," mused Lynn. She suddenly looked totally gobsmacked as a huge revelation came to her. "A circuit just like a train track in one continuous circle! Oh my Lord, what have we stumbled on to?"

The others were realizing too. Arthur continued the theorizing, hoping to implicate Mr Toppol even further.

"And a big-headed jerk with immense electrical expertise, and ego to match, would surely know how to store that energy," he said.

"The pieces in this puzzle are coming together, but we're not there yet," surmised Lawrence. "The Ghost Train, is it real? Why was the Underground constructed on leylines? And what the flipping heck has any of it to do with those confounded Rips in time?"

"And more importantly, why is Toppol still at large in our school, polluting the minds of our women?" snapped Arthur.

Lawrence and Lynn nodded in agreement. Mel nodded too, but with his bottom lip stuck out as he wasn't following any of this.

"We must investigate. Tonight. We have to find one of the entrances to the old Circle Line and see if the Underground track is still there," suggested Arthur, all the time watching as the fire in Lynn's eyes glowed brighter. Ask any other adult at eight o'clock on a Friday night to rush out with you and go on a fanciful investigation and they'd call a child psychologist. But not Mel and Lynn, they were two old fogies who'd never really grown up. They had no more maturity nor responsibility than the two lads and this is precisely why Arthur and Lawrence loved them so much.

"To the train station then," said Lynn.

"Yes, to the train station!" bellowed Arthur grandly. He pulled a face. "Why the train station, Lynn?"

"In London's Kings Cross there's a direct link between the mainline station and their Underground station. So you can hop off the overground train and hop on the Underground one. And vice versa. Ours worked the same way. And we know the overground station is still there."

"To the train station!" bellowed Arthur a second time. "The game's afoot!' Then under his breath he said, "Still afoot."

* * *

"HEALED THROUGH HUMILIATION" was the Cleveland Constabulary's new crime-fighting motto. The idea, unlike some of their other crime tackling initiatives*, was a good 'un. The theory was

---

* Namely their ridiculous idea of stopping motorists speeding by putting speed bumps every few metres on motorways and dual-carriageways.

that all persistent offenders would be made to do very silly things in public to belittle them, sap their confidence and set them on the right path. It was actually proving to be quite effective. If you were a 25-year-old male car thief and forced to dress like a little girl and stand in the corner of a busy shopping centre and think about what you'd done, you'd soon see the error of your ways. All the laughter from passing shoppers, the jeers, the finger-pointing and name-calling would frighten off anyone from re-offending.

Another idea of HTH was to make teenage offenders join the Boy Scouts and right now on this very Friday night, six 17- to 19-year-old bad lads were sitting round a campfire in Albion Wood, wearing scout uniforms that were ridiculously too small for them. Big Geoff, an ex-prison guard, was supervising them and he was not one to trifle with. Big Geoff was, as his name suggests, big. Huge. Colossal. There was a rumour he could pull the head off a horse with one arm, but had never had need to prove it, thank God.

The enormous, muscle-bound and stern-looking Geoff was making the bad lads sing very very silly campfire songs to make them feel even dafter than they already looked in their tiny uniforms. And by crikey was it working well. They cringed and closed their eyes as they sang such campfire songs as. . .

"FIND ME A BOG HOUSE ME WOGGLE'S
ON FIRE"
"HORSEY WENT TO LONDON AND CAME
BACK A MAYOR"
"BILLY'S SLEEPING BAG SMELLS LIKE
GYPSIES"
"I BURNT MY DADDY IN HIS DRINKING
SHED"
"OLD MAN RICKETS HAS LOST HIS PIG"
"FLIBBERTIGIBBET THE HALF DEAD TOAD"
"THERE'S A HOLE IN MY BOTTOM
(DEAR LIZA)"

They were just finishing another one and half-heartedly sang. . .

> *"Who's been doing all the poo poos?*
> *Who's been doing all the poo poos?*
> *I think it was you you.*
> *You did all the poo poos.*
> *Should have used the loo loo.*
> *Yes you've been doing all the poo poos."*

Big Geoff allowed them a short breather as he retuned his guitar.

"Big Geoff," said one of the wrong 'uns. "Please can we stop now? We've learnt our lessons."

"Over my dead body. And it's Mr Big Geoff to you, you little rodent. You'll sing until you drop," replied the large fellow.

"How about something to eat? We're totally Hank Marvin*," said another.

"Over my dead body."

"A cuppa from your flask?" said yet another lad hopefully.

"Over my dead body."

"Can we go to the pub after?" asked another lad.

"Over my dead body."

Then something odd happened. The air around them went very thin. The trees stopped moving. The flames of the fire stopped flickering and froze. And right above Big Geoff's head a split in the air appeared. It widened, showing twinkling beads of light inside. Mesmerized with fear, Big Geoff gaped up at the Rip as it slowly descended, encompassing his entire body. It only lasted a couple of seconds but it seemed like for ever. The bad lads were also mollified by the sight.

Then it vanished. But what was left behind was even more terrifying.

Big Geoff was dead. He was now the skeleton that he shouldn't have been for another forty years. He was still wearing his scout uniform, but it was old and tattered and in rags. The guitar he'd been holding had warped and rotted with age too. One of the bad lads reached over and prodded the skeleton which instantly fell apart into a heap of bones. The

---

* *Which meant they were "starving". Ironically, they were all also in the shadows too, but – like you – didn't get that particular gag.*

six lads were too shocked to speak for a moment, but soon saw the funny side. Then they. . .
– stopped singing silly songs
– had something to eat
– had a cuppa from Big Geoff's flask, and
– went to the pub.

And they did all of these things, quite literally, over Big Geoff's dead body.

CHAPTER
SIX

A rthur, Lawrence, Mel and Lynn were soon in their coats and on their way across Thornaby to its train station. Arthur had his deerstalker on together with a pipe and a magnifying glass that Lynn had bought him from the Oxfam shop that afternoon. And even though the magnifying glass was held together with sticky-tape and didn't actually have any glass in, and the pipe was made just to blow bubbles, the lad really felt like Conan-Doyle's legendary sleuth.

Mel and Lynn strolled in the warm dusky night. They held hands and occasionally stopped to kiss, much to the disgust of Arthur and Lawrence who were a good ten metres ahead.

"So what did Mr Wonderful say when he played that trick on you with the Ineffectualator gizmo?" asked Arthur.

"What do you mean, *what did he say*? He didn't say anything," replied Lawrence, screwing up his face.

"He did, he whispered something to you, I saw him. About me, was it? I can take it, you know. Just tell me. I bet he was calling me something like Gonk or Wassock or Doris or something. Is that what he said? It was, wasn't it? I bet it was Doris."

"Arthur, you're getting paranoid now. Even more paranoid than normal," sighed Lawrence.

Arthur thought for a second, then said, "I bet *he* calls me paranoid as well, doesn't he?"

Fairly soon the four were at Thornaby Station. Not that there was a station here. More like a platform and not a very pretty one at that. The council had once put a bench there. Had a big ceremony in honour of it with fireworks, marching bands and stuff. But by the time the big event was over somebody had swiped the bench, so they never bothered again. Now the station was desolate with only the occasional local train creeping up and, if the driver remembered, stopping.

The four of them looked around and pondered where the old entrance to the Underground station named Station Station may have been. There really wasn't anywhere to begin looking. To the left was the newly developed Teesdale Executive Site with its plush offices and expensive flats. Nothing there was under ten years old so that was a non-starter. To the right looked more hopeful. But wasn't. There were some very old buildings. One was a working men's club and the other was Thornaby Town Hall.*

* One was somewhere drunken loudmouths can complain about anything and
  everything, the other was a pub.

They'd have been there about the same time as the Underground, but would have been in constant use so it was unlikely they'd yield any secrets.

"This 1897 map may be our best bet," said Lynn, trying to find a point of reference by turning the folded map in every direction she could whilst surveying the surroundings. "Oh this is impossible, I've got less bearings than a ruddy Asda trolley."

"Hmmmm," said Lawrence. "Let's let logic decide. What would the greatest ever detective do in this situation?" He wiggled his eyebrows at Arthur.

"Scooby Doo*?" asked Arthur.

Lawrence, still doing the eyebrow thing, nodded up at the deerstalker atop his nut. "Oooh, Sherlock! Well, he'd probably say we should try and separate the improbable from the probable. For did not Holmes himself say, '*Once you have excluded the impossible then. . .*' erm '*. . .whatever remains must be. . .*' erm '*. . .the git what nicked my bike*'."

"Sherlock Holmes said that?" asked Mel, pulling a face.

"Yes," lied Arthur nervously. "In *The Case of the Belgravia Bike Thief*. Am I not right, Lawrence?' Lawrence shook his head. "Thank you, yes of course he did. I need to ponder this utilizing all my intellect and concentration. This is a three-pipe problem, but

---

* *The famous American talking-dog detective, not the cheap Australian version, Didgeri-Doo.*

seeing as I am out of washing-up liquid, I'll just have a nice sit down." He sat down on the platform cross-legged and chewed his pipe.

As Arthur pondered, the others watched the one-carriage shuttle to Saltburn trundle past them and keep on going.* After a few minutes, Arthur stood up and the others gathered round him to hear his decision borne out of intelligence and logic. Sheepishly Arthur said, "Let's just wander round and see what happens." So they did.

The four of them roamed around Thornaby checking thoroughly every clump of bushes, waste-land, bridge and abandoned building they came across for a forgotten door, a hatch, just a teensy clue. But after nearly three hours searching they'd found nothing at all helpful. Tell a lie, Mel found an old crisp packet from the early 1990s so they had a good chat about sweets and snacks you can't buy any more. Other than that nothing.

Then came the rumbling.

Very subtle at first.

Straight away they thought it to be vibrations from the dual-carriageway. It was by now approaching midnight and the streets and roads were nigh-on deserted, so any sound was carried much further than during the day.

But the rumble grew. And grew. And grew until the very ground beneath them seemed to swell and

---

* The driver did indeed forget to stop, even though he saw four people waiting.

undulate. The vibration passed beneath them and carried on at a steady rate.

"What is it?" gasped Mel anxiously, clinging on to Lynn for balance and comfort.

"It's the Ghost Train! It's got to be!" laughed Lawrence nervously.

"We must follow it, come on!" shouted Arthur.

"Get knotted!" snapped Mel. "That's the ruddy Ghost Train. It goes after dead people, living people don't go after *it*!"

"We're following it!" shouted Lynn.

And follow it they did. Down back streets, up front streets, across flower beds, over lawns and walls and office car parks, until they stopped outside a grim-looking disused timber yard on a small industrial estate in the very centre of Thornaby. The vibrations carried on under it without them. Surrounded by cracked concrete posts holding a rusted mesh fence, it was clear no one had bothered even breaking into the place in ages. It had a sign saying "*Woody's Wood. It's Good Wood. Well It Wood Be!*" and had a really bad faded drawing of a Pinocchio-type wooden boy smiling hideously.

"Well, it's not hard to see it was the chap in charge of advertising that sent this business down the bog," said Arthur.

Finding a stretch of wire-mesh fence that had given up on even being a fence any more, they stepped over it and into the timber yard. All around were badly stacked piles of planks in two rows. They walked down the centre of them towards a huge, rickety old building. It was quite a military-looking structure with massive sliding iron doors.

"Gosh, this must be one of the last remaining aircraft hangars in the area," commented Lynn. "Thornaby was a huge aerodrome for the RAF during the Second World War. When they moved out in the 1950s they sold all the old hangars, munitions buildings and officers' messes to private businesses."

Lynn was going to carry on talking, but she was getting wise to the others by now. She knew if she had and ended it with, "I don't suppose you want to listen to me going on," then they'd have done just that and walked on. She followed the others as they circled the building looking for clues or an entrance to the hangar.

"Now listen, you three," whispered Mel sternly. "I don't mind following some weird vibration thingy. That's the normal level of weirdness Arthur inflicts on us. But this, this is trespassing on private property. It's wrong, you hear?"

Arthur and the others nodded in solemn agreement, but instantly forgot what Mel had said when they spotted a door behind a big metal bin on wheels. They nudged it out of the way. The wooden doorframe had rotted away long ago (another bad advert for Woody's Wood) and fell through when Arthur kicked it once.

Inside the tall, dark and smelly building were more rows of wood, piled to the ceiling in stacks seven or eight metres high. To the far end of the warehouse was a small prefab hut, half decayed and fallen in on itself.

"Well, I hope you're happy," continued Mel. "We're now officially criminals and there's no sign of this wretched Ghost Train. Come on, let's go home."

The vibration came again, much much more intense as it seemed to bounce off the rusted aircraft-hangar walls. The entire structure resonated, shaking the huge stacks of wood dangerously. Arthur looked up at them, then down to the floor. He stomped his foot on it. *Concrete*, he thought. He glanced over at the prefab hut office. It seemed momentarily alive with vibration. He deduced by this that the ground wasn't as thick underneath it and gestured to the others to follow.

The vibrations slowly ceased.

Lynn said, "It's passed under us again. It's obvious the Ghost Train is running the Underground Circle Line."

"Therefore we're above the line. Therefore there may be a link down to it under this hut. I reckon the floor under this is wooden because the vibration was more intense here. Rip up the floor, everyone," said Arthur.

"No need," said Lawrence. "I've found a way in."

They spun round to see he was holding up a trapdoor. Under it was a ladder leading deep down into the Earth, but where only darkness should be, was illumination, some kind of light.

"This is odd, very very odd. Look at this hinge – it's new, not a bit of rust on it. The ladder too – it's new wood that. Someone's been using this opening and probably still is," said Mel, looking even more concerned. "I say we go and tell the police."

"Oh, and how do we explain how we found it, Mel?" asked Lynn exasperatedly. "We shouldn't be here in the first place."

"Lynn's right. We have to investigate," said Arthur bravely. "We should not flinch from the task ahead."

"I suppose not," said Mel, less than half-heartedly.

"Good lad, Mel, you go first."

"Oi! How come I go first, Arthur? You're the dashing young hero here."

"Get stuffed, there might be a mouse down there," said Arthur giving a girly shiver.

Reluctantly Mel led the way. He backed down the ladder followed by Lynn, then Lawrence, then Arthur. Down they climbed for a good thirty metres and the illumination grew brighter. Then they were there . . . on the Thornaby Underground.

CHAPTER
SEVEN

It was simply amazing.

A large tunnel with an arched roof, seven metres across where the station platform was. Below them were train tracks, three metres across from wall to wall, which ran in conjunction with the curve of the tunnel and disappeared to their left and right. The entire interior was illuminated by large ceiling lamps that looked like they should be gas-powered, but were electric. The walls were covered with shiny white tiles. Red tiles spelt out the word Mutznutts. The public entrance and exit stairway was bricked up. Now they could see where they were in relation to the platform and track they saw they had entered through some sort of service hatch in the ceiling.

"It's incredible. It's just as the legend says. A train station from the Victorian age," said Lynn.

They tried to take in everything, starting with the old-fashioned automatic ticket machine. It was craftsman-built and unused. It was sturdy and ornate and wouldn't have lasted two minutes without being vandalized on a modern train station. Arthur smirked at the adverts hand-painted on to the tiles with slogans you just couldn't get away with these days.

DRINK
Gulliver's
STOMACH BEER
ONLY FRENCH WOOPSIES
AND LITTLE GIRLS DON'T!

BAULDER-DASH
HORSE-DRAWN CABS
We'll get you there or by God
you can BALLY WELL WALK!

SERVANT PROBLEMS?
Use a Pimlico's Leather Strap.
Thrash some respect into
the blighters with a Pimlico's!
THAT'LL LEARN 'EM!

Johnny Walker's
THUNDERSTICK MATCHES

Warning: Thundersticks are highly
unpredictable and should only be
used by maids and snipes.

WIFE GAGS
Stop her nagging with a
GARSTANG'S silk wife gag.

Gentlemen's
Test-Me-Not-Trousers
with built-in spring-loaded finger
snap-traps to stop the pickpocketing
working classes doing what they do.

"So this is Mutznutts," said Lynn, examining her ancient tube map. "We must have followed the entire Circle Line above ground because the next one that way –" she gestured left – "is Station Station. If we kept going we'd then come to Bobby Boutique. I say we go that way and do the entire line, but this time under the ground. Presumably all the other five stations are sealed like this one so we'll need to come back here to get out."

"I say we get out of here now," said Mel, who was by now working himself up to a state of utter panic. "Supposing the Ghost Train really is running around this track? It comes for those who've died. Supposing whatever godless creature drives the blooming thing mistakes us for the recent dead and whisks us off to the afterlife! Or me at least. It's bound to be me, I'm the oldest one here! I'm nearer to death than any of you. Supposing—"

Mel stopped speaking when Lynn slapped his face.

"Calm down you silly old goat," she said. "There's no such thing as the Ghost Train. What we have here is real and tangible. There's an explanation for it."

"You're right, I suppose," admitted the old man, rubbing his cheek.

"Can I hit him next time, Lynn?" asked Arthur.

Lawrence looked at her map and said, "We should also look for an entrance to the Hub-office too. That's behind that wall there." He pointed to the wall across the track which had a massive section of it hidden behind a shut brass curtain.

"Hub-office?" asked Mel.

"Yeah, it was supposedly where all the Underground workers would be centred. Office staff, station masters, cleaners, service teams, that sort of thing. I'll bet there's some answers there all right."

The four walked gingerly along a thin service ridge which lined the tunnel.

They walked in single file, holding on to the tiled wall, never once daring to glance at the shiny metal tracks just thirty centimetres below them which, although silent, could have been alive with powerful electricity and certain death to the touch.

"I've heard loads of people have died because of the electric train tracks on Underground lines," said Arthur, trying to make conversation to ease the tension and oblivious to the fact he was making things worse. "Tramps and drunks mainly. They have a pee on the tracks and get electric shocks. It's true. The electricity arcs up the urine stream and into their –" he coughed – "you-know-whats and kills them dead."

Lynn politely said, "That's nice, Arthur, thank you for that, but we're possibly dangerously near a highly electrified track. Perhaps a change of subject might be better?"

Arthur nodded knowingly. "I get you, Lynn. Don't add to the tension, eh?"

They carried on for a few more steps. Then Arthur spoke again.

"Do you know the largest amounts of suicides are always on the Underground. It stands to reason, doesn't it? The speed those trains run. *Woosh. Splat.* Over in seconds."

Mel, still very jittery, was just about to call Arthur an incredibly rude name when he spotted something ahead. It was another platform, the Station Station station. But there was something even more astounding parked at that station. It was a train!

. The four of them carefully stepped on to the platform and walked along the train, eyeing it carefully. It was, like the rest of the Underground, Victorian by design and decor. Brass-plated with ornate bolted-on designs showing angels in flight and phoenixes rising from the flames. Another brass plaque read, "The Hiking Viking" and depicted a Viking with his thumb up next to the train itself. There were seven carriages with semi-frosted glass windows and tie-back curtains. Looking in, the four saw that where there had obviously once been seats, there were now bolted-in banks of big chunky storage batteries. Hundreds and hundreds of them in rows with masses of odd and fantastic-looking leads, plugs, wires and other confusing stuff billowing from them. The batteries were housed in all the carriages save for the final one, the driver's engine.

Arthur carefully peered in through the window and saw it was empty. He looked around and reached for the doorhandle. They stepped aboard the engine and noticed it too had curtains, crimson velvet ones hanging from expensive-looking brass poles. They gazed in wonder at the controls. At the front of the driver's cabin was a dashboard of levers, switches, dials, meters and other whatnots and thingummy-jigs. Underneath the dashboard was a large handle running on an arc-shaped track with numbers above it which Arthur presumed was the accelerator stick, it currently being at zero and the train being stationary.

"Curiouser and curiouser," said Mel.

"Hmm, you're right, Mel. I too feel like I've fallen through some hole and ended up like Alice In Wonderland," said Lynn.

"No, I was reading the nameplate. There, look." Mel pointed to a little plaque which read, CURIOUSER & CURIOUSER, MAKERS OF FINE DASHBOARDS. "They must have made the dashboard, do you reckon? Still going is Curiouser & Curiouser. They make fag machines now."

"There seems an awful lot of controls here for just a little engine, and one track to boot," said Arthur. "A most perplexing riddle."

"Indeed, Arthur, we must proceed with our investigation carefully," added Lawrence, "Lest we should upset any of this confounded technology."

Arthur nodded in agreement then said, "Wonder if this *is* the accelerator then," as he pushed the handle on the arced track to Level 5. Arthur's answer came swiftly and the four of them were jerked violently forward as the train shot backwards.

"Arthur, you twit!" snarled Mel, his face squashed near flat against the windscreen.

"Sorry," gasped Arthur, he too of flat phizog. "Damn thing must be in reverse!" They could feel how much electric power the machine had as it vibrated cleanly and perfectly. Back along the curve of track the train went and out of sight of Station Station. The last thing the four noticed was the open service shaft that had been directly under the train. And more importantly the shadow-clad figure of the man climbing up from the shaft and giving chase to the train in-between the tracks.

Back they flew faster and faster until Arthur gathered his wits and returned the lever to its zero position. With a really cool-sounding metallic *screeeeech!* the train came to rest directly opposite Mutznutts where they had entered the Underground.

"Did you see him? Did you see him too?" gasped Lawrence.

"We did, and he saw us. We nicked his flaming train for God's sake!" said Mel.

"Discretion would be the more sensible course of action here, chaps and chapess," suggested Arthur nervously. "Leg it."

And with that the four of them leapt off the train on to the platform and were back up the ladder like rats up a drainpipe. Back into the prefab office they scurried, out the hangar side-door and all the way home. They disappeared into the night, watched by a lone figure who had taken the same route they had but had stopped at the hangar perimeter fence. In the dark night the figure, wearing a Victorian frock coat and Gentlemen's Test-Me-Not-Trousers, tapped his chin, thinking hard. Turning on his heels he clipped the safety catch on his trouser pockets and took out a metal match box from which he withdrew a Walker's Thunderstick Match. Lighting the match he stepped back into the hangar and set about starting a blaze the like of which the good (and bad) folk of Thornaby had never seen before.

It was now half past one in the morning and Arthur and Lawrence were quietly entering Arthur's home, the house next door to Mel and Lynn's. The elderly couple were seeing them in. Lawrence slept over at Arthur's every Friday night and because Arthur's parents simply accepted their son would be out until God-knows-when doing odd things, they just let Lawrence do it too.*

"We'll come by tomorrow to discuss what we've seen," whispered Arthur.

Mel gave them the thumbs up and they all retired for the night, exhausted, but with their minds reeling.

---

* If only more grown-ups were this irresponsible – childhood would be a much jollier time.

CHAPTER
EIGHT

Saturday mornings, when Mel and Lynn were kids, meant rising early to play out in all weathers, or a trip to the pictures to see a Gary Cooper western or a Buster Crabbe sci-fi series. In the twenty-first century kids seldom flopped out of bed before eleven o'clock to watch some badly written Saturday morning kids' show.

Not so Arthur and Lawrence. They were always up, dressed and out of the house by half past eight. Then they'd go next door to Mel's and watch badly written Saturday morning telly until they could think of something better to do.

Not so today. Mel and Lynn hastily ushered the two lads into the living room to show them an ongoing local news report live from the scene of a massive fire on a small industrial estate in Thornaby. Their four jaws collectively dropped to see it was the old RAF hangar where Woody's Wood had been, now nothing more than a massive heap of charred wood and blackened twisted metal. Donning their coats they were on the scene faster than fat lasses to a bun shop.

The crowds were out already. There's nothing like a disaster to get people's curiosity going. Just give the general public a car crash, a collapsed bridge or a raging fire and they're happy.*

More exciting was the appearance of a top news deity – Tyne-Tees Television's Mr Pontop Pike, no less. Pontop was giving an on-the-spot report to camera when the four arrived and had pushed through the crowd sufficiently to see what was going on. Where the once huge hangar had stood was now carnage. What the German Luftwaffe failed to do in the Second Big One, some loony with a match had done in minutes. Arthur, Lawrence and Lynn were busy discussing the serious implications this threw up in relation to their discovery.

Mel, on the other hand, was stood at the front of the crowd behind Pontop Pike waving and pulling stupid faces into the camera. The newscaster caught glimpses of the silly old man behind him on the monitor and tried to blank him out with a series of uncomfortable postures, but Mel always found another gap to do another face through.

"It's obvious whomever was in the tunnel last night is up to no good. Why else would they deliberately destroy the hangar," reasoned Arthur. "We have to dig deeper, but we need to be astute

---

* You can bet some tosspot, goatee-beard-wearing cable-TV exec somewhere has already thought up "The Tragedy Channel". You just wait.

and alert at all times. We need a plan that is sharper than Moriarty's tie-pin."

"One that doesn't involve the police, though," pleaded Lynn. "They wouldn't understand. Besides, I'm still wanted by the rozzers, remember."

"Oh yeah. All that direct action for the environment stuff you've done," said Lawrence, nodding thoughtfully.

"And the nicking. Yeah."

"What?"

"Oh sorry, that slipped out," said Lynn. "Look, Arthur, you might hate me for this but I think this Mr Toppol might be able to help us out."

"I agree," said Lawrence. "His ancestor created that Underground. He must have some idea what's going on."

"Exactly," snapped Arthur angrily. "Leering Lesta is related to long dead loony Elle Toppol. Insanity runs in their family. Which is why, for one, he's unfit to teach, and secondly he's not to be trusted."

"Arthur, remember the bigger picture," said Lawrence. "This goes beyond your jealousy. You have to put aside your feelings of hurt just because Gwen's got a crush on Toppol. For was it not Sherlock Holmes himself who said, *'The needs of the many outweigh the needs of the few'*." Lawrence gave Arthur a humbling look.

"Was it knackers. That was Mr Spock in *The Wrath of Khan*. Don't try and confuse me with famous sci-fi quotes, mate," shouted Arthur.

Lawrence swore to himself. When would he realize that Arthur's head was full of more useless trivia than his.

From out of the crowd stepped Gwen. "Hi Arthur, how are you today?" She smiled sheepishly and looked to the ground, embarrassed. She was wearing a short skirt and knee-length leather boots and Arthur had to fight the drooling pangs he felt inside to snub her. Mustering all his dignity, which wasn't much when she had leather boots on, he forced himself to turn his back on her.

"OK, OK, I deserve that. I was out of order yesterday. I didn't mean what I said. You're not a silly little boy. Well, actually you are, but you're also a kind and considerate young man and don't deserve to be spoken to like that. I could never hate someone like you."

Arthur excitedly mouthed the word "Yes" to himself then regained a steely gaze. He turned to look at her.

"I'd do anything to make it up to you," said Gwen.

"Really?" said Arthur, now smiling widely. "Can I see you naked then?"

Pontop wrapped up his live report from the Thornaby fire and turned to Mel who had his tongue out, his ears pulled and his eyes screwed up. (He was having the time of his life.)

"You there, the buffoon," said the newscaster sternly. He shouted, "Is there someone who looks after you?"

"Eh?" replied Mel, "I'm not senile, you know."

"Ah, denial, that's the first sign. Tell you what, old person, seeing as you like being on telly, how about I interview you for a pre-record item to go in tonight's news?"

"You what? Yes, all right then!" said Mel, clapping his hands with sheer glee.

"And would you do all your amusing faces and things, to pep the item up?" asked Pontop.

"Try and stop me. It'll be great. I can do loads, you know. Watch this." Mel pulled another stupid face. "Oh Mr Pike, this is fantastic. Thanks."

"Oh, no need to thank me," said Pontop smiling. "I'm lying."

And with that the newscaster walked away from the bewildered-looking Mel to watch the other attraction that was stealing the limelight from the fire. A 15-year-old girl was beating the living breakfast out of a 13-year-old boy whom she had pinned to the ground sitting astride his chest. Arthur screamed as Gwen rained down blows upon him. In between punches Arthur caught glimpses of her pants which in no small way took his mind off the searing pain in his face and neck.

Lynn looked down at Lawrence and sighed. "We have a lot of work to do, Lawrence."

* * *

Martin Casson was what psychiatrists expertly termed "a child in need of a punch". He was by far the most hyperactive and mischievous ten-year-old you could ever have the misfortune to meet. Not necessarily evil, just completely destructive and badly behaved. His parents despaired of him and had even run away from home on three separate occasions. Social workers always managed to catch up with the distraught pair and send them back to their perpetual nightmare.

Martin had begun his Saturday morning like every other day. Some light mischief in the morning, random relaxed disobedience around lunchtime, followed by some rigorous waywardness in the afternoon.

And at night, all hell would break loose!

Today he awoke at six o'clock, had a wee, then got up. He then took an electric razor to the dog and shaved "*I ama kat*" in its fur. After breakfast, or rather putting Frosties and milk in his dad's petrol tank, Martin was about to go back into the house to play with some matches when he noticed a headline in the paper on the carpet by the front door. He was utterly stunned by two things. Firstly it was a Sunday newspaper, despite the fact it was definitely Saturday. Secondly it had his picture on the front and a headline which read. . .

AWFUL LITTLE BOY BEHEADS FAMILY FOR A LAUGH!

Martin choked and gagged with terror. Sheer panic and horrendous confusion made his legs buckle beneath him. He could barely breathe.

"I never did that! I never did! It's Saturday not Sunday and I never chopped off Mum and Dad's heads coz I would have remembered!" he yelled.

Then he did remember something – the Time Rips everyone had been going on about. The slashes in the air through which people had experienced events from the past and future. Yes, everyone knew about them! Mum and Dad even told him about them every time Martin had stopped for meals in-between bouts of mischief!

Oh no, no no no no no no, this can't be real! Was he actually experiencing one now? Had he really moved forward 24 hours to a time after he'd gone too far? After he'd he pushed back the boundaries of naughtiness to such an extent that he'd actually chopped off his parents' heads for a laugh?

He dropped the paper and ran into the kitchen where Mum and Dad should be taking breakfast. And they were there all right – well, bits of them.

Their heads!

Mouths gaping, eyes bulging, their severed heads sat on the kitchen table. Just plonked there like some hellish salt and pepper pots. Standing looking mournfully at the heads were his aunts, uncles, grandparents and elder cousins. They were all wearing black arm bands and crying. They all slowly pointed at him and let out one long continuous wail: "Aaaaaaaaaaaaaaaaaaaaaaaaaawwwwwwwwwwwwww wwwwwwwwwwww."

On and on it went. Then they clapped in perfect timing. Two claps. One. Two claps. One.

Martin felt his heart and brain would burst with the horror of the scene. He covered his ears and screamed, "I didn't! I didn't do it! I swear!" But the wailing and the clapping went on.

He turned to flee, but ran head-first into something black. It was a uniform. A police uniform with a very stern-looking white-haired policeman inside it, glaring unsympathetically down at him. He put his hand on Martin's shoulder and . . . sang.

(To the tune of Queen's "We Will Rock You")
Martin you're a bad lad – did a wicked thing:
Thought it didn't matter what the grown-ups say.
Mix you shouldn't oughta
Family and slaughter.
Took a carving knife and made 'em both much
*   shorter.*
I tell yer,
I will, I will, nick you!
I will, I will, nick you!

Over and over he sang the last line as the wailing and clapping continued.

Martin, by now almost passing out with mental confusion, ran to the front door, but it was locked. The party of relatives, led by the singing policeman, filed out of the kitchen towards him. Martin screamed louder and darted upstairs to the only place anyone is ever really safe – under the duvet. Shivering with fear, trying to dodge the widdle on the mattress, he curled up into a ball and tried to listen over the deafening sound of his own racing heart.

The wailing and clapping was no more. It had stopped.

But then there came a sound. Footsteps. Two sets. Then the bedroom door-handle turned and people entered. They walked towards the bed. He felt a hand take the duvet. It was wrenched off him and he expected to see the entire Stockton police force ready to take him away. Instead, there stood . . . Mum and Dad. Both calm, in one piece, and smiling.

"You OK, son?" asked Mum.

"We heard you scream," added Dad.

Martin threw up and passed out.

A few minutes later he had been calmed down sufficiently to tell them what had happened and they agreed he must have fallen through a Time Rip. Luckily, though, he must have somehow managed to get back to the present before he'd done any head-lopping-mischief. Martin was so relieved. He hugged his Mum and Dad and cried and cried, vowing from that moment on he would never do anything naughty again. He had been given a glimpse into a very dark and disturbing future and now he could change it for the better. And he meant it. He was a reformed lad.

Dad left him cuddling Mum and telling her how much he loved her and how much nicer her head was on her shoulders.

Downstairs, Dad stepped into the kitchen and said, "It worked."

There was a collective sigh of relief from the family members as they took off their armbands and went home. The singing policeman, Chief Inspector Mark Robertson, patted Dad on the shoulder and said, "The short sharp shock treatment, Mr Casson. Cruel to be kind. I'm sorry the lad had to go through such a deception."

"I'm not," said Dad. "I've still got a tankful of cereal to deal with. But it's a small price to pay now our troubles are over. Hey, that trick with the fake table was amazing."

The police officer was folding up the bogus kitchen table. "My brother uses it in his amateur magic shows for kids' parties. There's nothing like a severed head popping out of a kid's birthday cake to get the party going," laughed the rozzer.

"Thank you, Chief Inspector Robertson. We owe you everything."

"Just keep singing, Mr Casson. Never stop singing."

"Oooh, you'd better take your newspaper too. It looks very real," said Dad.

"You can do anything with a good printer these days. Ta-ra."

And with that, the jolly copper put on his copper

topper and sneaked out the back door, happy in the knowledge another naughty person had been set on the path of righteousness.

* * *

Back at Mel and Lynn's house, Gwen was filled in with the events of the previous night. Arthur was having plasters applied to his face as he'd been well and truly filled in too. Although he was happy that Gwen was talking to him again.

"Amazing. Absolutely amazing," said Gwen. "And I agree, Mr Toppol is the best person to talk to first." She checked her watch. "I was going to go to Middlesbrough and meet the girls at Shake and Make Up*, but this is far more important. We can go and see him straight away."

"No!" piped up Arthur, pushing Lynn's hand aside. "On the grounds that . . . that . . . that—"

"It's Saturday?" chipped in Lawrence, trying to finish Arthur's sentence for him.

"No, on the grounds that he's a complete creep and we all hate him."

"*You* hate him, Arthur. We don't. Mel and Lynn don't even know him," said Gwen.

"They'd hate him if they met him, wouldn't you?" replied Arthur, looking expectantly at Mel and Lynn. The couple fumbled for an answer that was diplomatic to both Gwen and Arthur, but couldn't find one.

* A girly shop in the Boro where chicks can buy eyeliners and lipsticks and stuff AND have a cool milk drink. Silly really.

"Yup," they replied in unison.

"See. And Lawrence hates him too, don't you?" It was the young lad's turn to grope for an answer that wouldn't upset Arthur or his own big sister.

"I'm really starting to, honest. But I think we should go and see him to suss him out more. See if he really is the swine I'm honestly starting to think he is."

"This is fair comment," decided Arthur. "But we can't today because school's shut."

"It's OK. I know where he lives. We can go to his house," said Gwen.

Arthur leapt to his feet and shouted, "You tart! What the hell are you doing going to that man's house alone? He isn't called Lesta The Molester for nothing, you know!"

"Yes he is, Arthur. *You* made that up, remember. And besides, there's always about twenty of us. He holds extra meetings of the science club on Saturday and Sunday afternoons. It's all innocent learning and not entirely suspect."

"Sounds perverted to me," sneered Arthur.

* * *

As it was Saturday Mel and Lynn took their weekly shopping trip to the supermarket, and as they were paying by debit card they wore their home-made "*No I do not want flamin' cash-back*" T-shirts*.

Gwen and Lawrence had convinced Arthur they

* *A little joke for you adults out there.*

93

wanted to talk to Mr Toppol in stern and scornful voices and he seemed happy with that.

Mr Toppol lived in a very nice house at the beginning of the stunningly beautiful Thornaby Green which overlooked a crook in the River Tees called Horseshoe Bend. When the three came to call upon him he was sat at a nice patio table with sunglasses on reading a novel by H G Wells.

How like him to improve his mind in his spare time, thought Gwen.

What a poof, thought Arthur.

CHAPTER
NINE

The three kids sat watching the brilliant sunshine glint off the pollution in the river. Mr Toppol came back on to the veranda with a trayful of Cokes.

"Now this really is a splendid start to one's weekend, isn't it. A visit from some good chums and the knowledge that Gwen and Arthur are back on speaking terms," said Mr Toppol with a jolly smile.

Arthur sniffed the glass of Coke he had been given, put it back down and took Mr Toppol's instead.

"We found the Thornaby Underground last night, Toppol," he said watching the teacher's face carefully for his reaction. "It's real."

Lawrence nodded, blowing bubbles in his drink through a straw.

"You have got to be kidding me! The Underground's an urban myth, isn't it?" said the teacher, looking genuinely taken aback.

"We saw it, and the Ghost Train. Except it's not a ghost, it's real. A genuine train from the last century.

And we saw somebody else down there and it's that person, we think, who covered his tracks by destroying the aircraft hangar, so we could never go back."

"Whoa whoa whoa, slow down, Lawrence. That fire on the news was connected to you finding the Underground?' Mr Toppol looked to Gwen for help.

"Sir, Arthur and my brother are many things, mostly stupid things, but they are not liars. If they say this is what happened then it surely did."

Arthur's chest swelled with pride and he put his arm round Gwen in gratitude and comradeship. She brushed him off and thumped him giving him a dead leg. Arthur fell forward, banged his head on the table and disappeared under it.

"That's good enough for me, Gwen. OK, we need to investigate further. We have to find another entrance to the tunnel," said Mr Toppol.

Lawrence produced Lynn's oldest map with the Circle Line drawn on it.

"This is what we've learned so far," said the young 'un. "We know Mutznutts is blocked by the burnt-out hangar. The next one is Station Station, where the train was parked, but there's no entrance above that at Thornaby Station. We know that for sure."

"What's this area now? Over here." Mr Toppol pointed to another station and looked hard at it. "Dead Dobbins."

"That's where our school is now, dur," said Arthur sarcastically, still under the table.

"Are you looking up my skirt, Arthur?" snapped Gwen.

Arthur jumped back into his seat and said, "No! I was looking at the welding on this patio set actually. Sub-standard."

"I wonder," said Mr Toppol, thinking hard. "The Bassleton boiler room goes pretty deep below floor level and they're refurbishing the pipes in there at the moment. If we could gain access to it we'd be able to have a ferret around, dig even deeper and see if there's some remaining access point from the old station. I mean, you never know."

"Who'd have thought we'd have found the one in the hangar," added Lawrence.

"Yes yes, all very interesting, but it's Saturday – the school's closed," said Arthur, sighing.

"Not for me, it isn't. I'm a teacher, remember. I have keys. But we'll need to be discreet about this. So please, not a word to anyone, OK?" Gwen and Lawrence agreed and after a brief pause Arthur did too.

"Great. Now give me a couple of minutes to make a few calls. I'll have to cancel today's science club."

Mr Toppol disappeared into his house and Arthur flicked the V sign at his back, so Gwen poked him in the eye.

* * *

Gwen loved Mr Toppol's car. It was so him, she thought.

97

Arthur hated Mr Toppol's car. It was so him, he thought.

"How's a teacher afford a brand new convertible sports car, Toppol?" he demanded as they drove through the sun-blessed streets of Thornaby.

Gwen swung round from the front passenger seat and gave Arthur a fierce look.

"Don't be rude, Arthur, what's it got to do with you!" she snapped.

"It's a fair question, Gwen. I found that my late great-great-grandfather had a few bonds and shares tucked away he never told anyone about. They'd matured in the years since he died and I cashed them in. That's the ticket, you see, chaps. Invest for your future. Always pays to think ahead."

They drew up at the school gates and Mr Toppol unlocked them, drove in and re-locked them. He parked the car in between the school and one of the huts to hide it from view as much as possible. He unlocked the wooden door to the boiler-room and ushered the three kids in.

It was dark and smelly in there. Pipes and gauges and boilers and things were everywhere. To the far end of the five by three metre room was a section of the floor that had been dug up and covered with a tarpaulin. Mr Toppol rolled it to one side and under it was a wooden hatch.

"Is this similar to the one you saw in the hangar?" asked the teacher.

"Do telephone boxes smell of wee?" exclaimed Lawrence. "It's exactly like it."

"Bit of a coincidence, them putting new pipes in here just when some loony's up to no good in the Underground again, isn't it, Toppol?" asked Arthur, eyeing the tarpaulin suspiciously.

"Very strange, isn't it. Whomever it is has probably taken advantage of the legitimate council work being done here to uncover some sort of duct into the Underground. Let's have a gander, shall we."

Mr Toppol gingerly lifted the hatch and the four of them gasped in unison. In it was the top of a ladder, much the same as the one in the hangar, and it too disappeared down into the Earth. Light came up from the hole.

"Come on, let's go," said Lawrence.

"Yes, that's exactly what *he'd* like us to do," said Arthur grandly, narrowing his eyes at Mr Toppol. "Wouldn't you, sir?"

"That's exactly what we're not doing. It's too dangerous. We are going straight to the police. This instant."

"Oh," said Arthur dejectedly.

"Oh please, Lesta, can we just take a peek first?" pleaded Gwen.

"No, sorry, Gwen, I've abused my position enough already. I cannot risk your safety too. Am I correct, Arthur?"

"Chick chick chick chick chicken, lay a little egg for me," sang Arthur mockingly at Mr Toppol. "Me and him went down there and we're just kids. Sheesh, absolutely everyone's right about you, Toppol, you're all mouth and trousers."

Mr Toppol sighed and thought for a second.

"OK, one quick look then we're back up and straight to the authorities, OK?"

And down they climbed, Mr Toppol leading the way. Arthur demanded that he should go just before Gwen for safety's sake, but she refused because she knew he only wanted to look up her skirt again.

Dead Dobbins was almost exactly like the Mutznutts and Station Station stations. Gwen and Mr Toppol were flabbergasted trying to take it all in. The old ticket machine, the advertisements. There was even a drinks machine at this one selling tots of brandy, whiskey and rum. The sign read. . .

Shuttington's One-Shot-Shut-Ups

Keep noisy toddlers, infants and babies silent with a Shuttington's.
In three delicious 45% proof flavours.

1d each

"Listen, can you hear something?" whispered Lawrence, hushing the others.

They listened hard.

Yes. There was definitely a sound coming from up the track to their right, but it curved out of sight so it was impossible to see where it was coming from. It was like the sound of distant machines working. The scraping of metal on metal and occasional hammering. Somewhere along the line people were working. But who and on what?

Led by Arthur, they mounted the thin service ledge and shuffled on for a good ten minutes. Arthur stopped them as he saw it first.

The train parked at Hobbler's End Station.

"Great Scott, look. There's people down there too. Observe, Lawrence!"

Sure enough there were. All they could make out of them was that they were wearing white robes with hoods covering their heads and faces. There were about nine of them moving slowly and laboriously, toiling like robots. They were taking panels off the train and tinkering with its workings. Some were walking in and out of the carriages, removing the battery cells and handing them to others who were walking out of sight with them. Some were on the track hammering the rails as others buffed the metal track with odd, purpose-built hand-held machines.

"What are they?" whispered Gwen.

"Morlocks?" offered Lawrence.

"No, they're human. Small humans!" Arthur gasped. "Mole people!"

"Or perhaps just kids, Arthur. Isn't that what small humans are?" said Gwen.

"Mole kids then?"

"But look at the way they're working," said Lawrence. "Handling those intricate batteries and machinery. No kid has skills and knowledge like that, human or mole-like."

"Clever mole kids?" mused Arthur.

"What exactly is a flaming mole kid? God, you two really are annoyingly stupid sometimes," snapped Gwen.

"Yes, I think this has gone on long enough, children," said Mr Toppol loudly.

Arthur turned to face him and noticed he no longer wore that aggravating, simpering look which so obviously said, "*I only want you to like me.*" He looked quite the serious chap. Arthur also noticed he was reaching into his pocket.

"You're right," said Gwen. We had better get back above ground and inform the police. Oh, we'll need Mel and Lynn to come with us too, sir – sorry, *Lesta.*"

Mr Toppol suddenly looked puzzled.

"Who are Mel and Lynn?" he asked.

"Friends of ours. They were with us last night," said Lawrence, without turning round. "They're old."

"What are you doing, Top—"

Arthur stopped talking and froze with sheer panic as behind them, stood between the tracks, was a figure in a white robe, also hooded. But this figure was not small like the others, it was adult-sized and holding as nasty a looking gun as you've ever seen. A cross between a highwayman's flintlock and a

102

machine-gun pistol. Just behind the figure was an open hatch between the tracks from where it must have silently emerged.

The others followed Arthur's terrified gaze and all saw the gun-toting figure too. Without seeming to think, Mr Toppol snarled angrily and leapt on the figure and they both fell to the ground beneath the tracks, wrestling madly.

"Get out of here quickly! Back to Dead Dobbins!" screamed Mr Toppol.

With utter terror the three kids began back-tracking on the ledge, but their progress was slow.

"Jump in-between the tracks, they're not electrified!" added Mr Toppol as he fought. Arthur jumped in between the tracks and ran like hell. Lawrence jumped next, then Gwen, letting out a long shaky girly yell, rushing to catch the two lads up.

They ran on.

Arthur looked ahead of them and saw Dead Dobbins but a stone's throw away. But to his horror, he also saw two of the smaller hooded figures coming towards them. The ladder leading up to the boiler room was in-between the oncoming pursuers and the good guys, meaning the good guys had to get to it first. Speeding up as much as he could Arthur reached the ladder just seconds before the hooded figures did. Grabbing on to the rungs he stopped his upper body dead and kicked his legs forward, jabbing a heel of each of his shoes into the chests of the hooded figures. They were knocked back into a flailing heap, cracking their heads on the metal tracks, and each other, as they went. They weren't unconscious, but dazed enough to buy Arthur and co some time.* Arthur grabbed Lawrence by the hips and lifted him up against the ladder to give him a few rungs start. The lad took good advantage of it and scurried up out of sight. Arthur grabbed Gwen's hand for her to go next.

"No!" she said and pulled her hand back.

"Oh for crying out loud, you damnable female, I won't look up your skirt!" snapped Arthur.

"No, I must go back for Lesta, I simply must!"

"Gwen, he's a grown man. He can fight for himself. We have to get out of here, there's too many of them!"

"I can't leave him, Arthur. I love him!" This was like a knife though Arthur's heart.

"Of all the lousy times to spring that one on me, you rotten cow!" he seethed.

"Arthur, go quickly!" came the voice of Mr Toppol as he staggered round the bend. He had blood on his T-shirt and looked exhausted. Close behind was the hooded man and behind him were the smaller hooded people. Satisfied that Gwen would now mount the ladder, Arthur began climbing. He took a quick look down and saw that Gwen wasn't even

---

* It's only in vintage TV shows like Dr Who and Blake's Seven that people get knocked out with one blow. Not in real life. Unless they're very very old, that is.

holding the rungs. She was crying hysterically, gesturing to Mr Toppol to hurry up. She seemed to suddenly calm down when Mr Toppol reached her. Now, sure that Gwen would follow, Arthur doubled his pace. He shouted down, "Move it, woman! Mr Wonderful is right behind you now!"

He emerged in the boiler room where Lawrence was in a heap gasping for breath.

"Where's Gwe—" Lawrence tried to ask, but the sound of a single gunshot rang out in the tunnel. The two of them looked in horror at one another, freezing as their minds threw up terrifying scenarios. They both sprang towards the ladder to go back down, but someone was coming up.

"Gwen!" yelled Arthur.

"No, it's me. Lesta!" Mr Toppol came up out of the hole and collapsed half out of it. He was nursing his shoulder which was gushing with blood. "I'm shot!"

"Oh thank God for that," sighed Arthur. "I thought it was Gwen."

"No, they took her. The smaller ones. There were too many of them. I tried to save her, but the larger one fired upon me!"

"They have my Gwen? Confound them! I'll sort this! I'll box their ears, but I can't promise to strictly adhere to the Marquess of Queenberry's rules," said Arthur, determinedly holding up his clenched fists. "I am far too incandescent with rage to remain gentlemanly!"

"No! There's too many of them!" said Lesta.

"And you can't fight, Arthur. Remember?" added Lawrence.

"Drat. I forgot about that," said Arthur, dropping his fists. "I'm going anyway." He made for the ladder. Mr Toppol stopped him.

"Arthur, you'll be killed instantly. You're no use to her dead, man! Besides, look at me, Arthur. I'm losing a lot of blood. We need to get help. This Mel and Lynn you spoke of. Trust me, lads, it's the only way!" Before the two could argue any further, Mr Toppol ushered them outside to his car. He tossed the keys to Arthur and said, "Drive."

Confused and bewildered, Arthur got in the driver's seat. Lawrence leapt into the back, wiping tears of fear and frustration from his face. Mr Toppol, now in the passenger seat, reached over and inserted the keys and started the engine. "You must have a basic idea. Put it in first gear and gently release the clutch whilst deploying the accelerator pedal. Quick, Arthur, get us out of here."

"I can't drive a car!" said Arthur, his voice quivering. "You do it."

"I'm in too much pain! You can do it, Arthur, I believe in you!"

He really should have listened to Arthur because, although operating the foot pedals neatly, Arthur completely forgot to even touch the steering wheel and crashed the left side of the car into the wall wrenching off the wing, indicator and mirror.

CHAPTER TEN

M r Toppol hadn't wanted to go to hospital on the grounds they'd ask too many questions about a bullet wound, so they went straight to Mel and Lynn's house.

It was now two hours later and the teacher lay on Mel's settee with a neatly applied dressing to his injured shoulder. Lynn had managed to extract the small slug and patch up the young teacher without too much fuss and pain. A certain amount of vomiting and fainting had occurred, but this was only Mel who really hated the sight of blood. Both he and Lynn had been told of the afternoon's events and the two aged ones fumbled for some kind of reason for it all.

"If it hadn't have been for sir, here, we'd have all been captured by those hooded little fiends," said Lawrence.

"Yes. I suppose I was wrong about you," said Arthur, a tad half-heartedly. "I apologize for my former rudeness and suspicion. I'm ashamed I fell into the old red herring trap. You're a noble man, Mr Toppol."

The teacher looked genuinely touched.

"Arthur, you called me Mr Toppol," he said, smiling.

"Sorry, Lesta," added Arthur, patting Mr Toppol's bad shoulder as hard as he could. The teacher gritted his teeth in pain.

"Well, it's not over yet, lads," said Mel. "We've got to get the police involved. It's kidnapping now, not to mention attempted murder."

"I agree," said Lynn.

"I also, but I think we may have a hard time convincing the constabulary," said the teacher. "You see –" Mr Toppol thought for a second, trying to find the right words. "You see, I think I know the man I fought with. What am I saying, I do know him. What I mean is, I know of him. I saw his face. It was Elle Toppol."

A hushed silence rang out for a moment.

"But that's impossible. He's been dead nearly a hundred years," said Lawrence, pulling a face equal in incredulity to the others'.

"I saw him, Lawrence, under the hood during the scuffle. He looked just like me. As young as me, thirty-something, when by rights he should look that plus a hundred years."

"Elle Toppol, the bloke who built the Underground? But he died in 1908. He's buried in Thornaby Cemetery," mused Lynn.

"If it wasn't him then I have a twin brother – which, good lady, I am sure I do not."

"Perhaps it's the low oxygen levels in the ground or something. You know, being that low under the Earth all this time. Maybe it's somehow halted the ageing process," reasoned Arthur.

Again genuinely impressed, Mr Toppol blinked at Arthur.

"Excellent reasoning, Arthur."

"I mean, stranger things have happened on *Star Trek*, haven't they."

Mr Toppol's look of being genuinely impressed faded a little.

"I have a theory that is as mad as a hen on Prozac, but lady and gentlemen, please give it some thought," said Mr Toppol. ". . .Time travel."

"You mean he's come through one of the Time Rips?" said Lawrence.

"I fear he's responsible for these Time Rips, Lawrence. Allow me to explain. It's a shameful family secret that my great-great-grandfather was insane. Ingenious, but unbalanced. He was two people. A 'split personality' they'd term it these days. On the one hand he was the nice ordinary businessman who owned shops and factories and tinkered with inventions. His biggest claim to fame was to be the Thornaby Underground which would fuse his money-making talent with his inventing skills. He designed a new form of train that could run on electricity whilst the southerners were still playing with underground steam engines. He was years ahead of them. To prove he could do it he commissioned the Underground Circle Line. But, as I said, he had another side, a darker side. A part of him that hated society, hated technology."

"Blimey, I bet he had some proper barneys with himself then," suggested Lawrence.

"That's more than likely. He formed the Cult of Temporal Renewal and tried to indoctrinate anyone daft enough to listen to him."

Mel was getting lost. "What's Temporary Removal when it's at home?"

"Temporal Renewal, Mel. He thought science had gone too far and wanted to transport every living thing back to the Stone Age. Not machines or buildings, just every living thing on the planet."

"What a fruitcake," said Arthur, popping his pipe into his mouth and stepping over to the window. He gazed out and soon became lost in thought.

"Nuttier than a fruitcake, Arthur, far nuttier," sighed Mr Toppol. "The story goes he never had any intention of opening the Underground to the public and closed it before it opened. Claimed he had it filled in. That's why when the eerie noises were heard at night the legend of the Ghost Train began. But they stopped in 1908 when he died."

"I know! I know that, I found that out, didn't I, Arthur?" yelped Lawrence excitedly.

Arthur remained staring at the garden and made a subtle *harumpf* noise.

"From what you've told me, I can only deduce

that my ancestor spent the years from 1900 to 1908 perfecting his Time Train before attempting it."

"What?" asked Lawrence. "He actually tried to send humanity back to the Stone Age?"

"Yes. I believe something went terribly wrong and he reappeared in this time 97 years later by mistake. What do you think of that?"

There was a pause. Lawrence lifted his hand as though hailing a cab.

"Straightjacket for Mr Toppol," he said.

Mel and Lynn laughed and even Mr Toppol sniggered, although it hurt his shoulder. Arthur remained silent.

Lynn spoke next.

"I actually think there could be something in it. Remember what we said the other day, that the stations on the Underground are all built on the three leylines."

"Good grief, really?" gasped Mr Toppol. "Then that's how he's powered it. Natural electro-magnetic energy. Wow. Ingenious. And, I'll bet these Rips in time are some kind of residual side effect from his temporal monkey business."

"I made that connection too!" yelped Lawrence excitedly. "Didn't I, Arthur? In the library. Tell them."

"Hmmmm," said the young sleuth in response to the younger sleuth.

"If you're right, then he still could be trying to send us all back to the Stone Age," said Lynn.

"Indeed. In the time since the Ghost Train noises

returned I'll wager he's managed to store enough temporal energy for a second attempt," said Mr Toppol, thinking hard.

"That does it. We have to go and stop him. He has that power at his fingertips right now," said Lawrence. He gulped. "And my big sis is down there with him."

"Shouldn't we get the police involved, like you said, Lynn?" asked Mr Toppol nervously.

"By the time we convince them of the story, one of two things might have happened," reasoned Lynn. "Firstly, Gwen might be dead. Secondly, we could be living in a ruddy cave complaining about our noisy neighbours who happen to be a gang of Neanderthal ape-beasts."

"Oh God," gulped Lawrence again, remembering the cavemen who mugged him in the toilets. "Not those hairy so-and-sos again."

There was a long pause. Arthur turned and spoke.

"You lot must try and convince the police. I alone must go and rescue Gwen." His tone was neither the bumbling weird kid the others knew so well, nor that of the upper class, razor-minded detective which he had adopted of late. Arthur spoke with a direct sincerity that was both calm and calculated. "It's bad enough the girl I worship is in danger. I am not about to put the other people I love in the same peril."

There was a long and thoughtful pause as the others fumbled for an answer.

"I don't love you, Toppol, I just like you. So you can come if you like."

The moment was suddenly gone. Mr Toppol got to his feet.

"I'm with you, Arthur."

Lawrence stepped up to Arthur and looked him in the eye.

"You need me, old chap, a Holmes without a Watson is not a happy Holmes. Besides, my big sis is down there and Mam'll knack me if I go home without her."

Arthur smiled at his young chum. "Lawrence, you have the heart of a lion."

Lynn got to her feet and stood next to Arthur.

"And you can't have a scrap without me, Arth. Come on, let's kick some Victorian bottom."

"Well, I might be thicker than a giant's greenie 'cause I aren't following any of this, but even I can see we have to go back down that Underground and sort this mess out," said Mel.

Nobody could disagree with that. Or the bit about needing to go back down into the Underground either. So the five of them walked out of the house to where Mr Toppol's damaged car was parked.

"Mel, I fear I am still not fit to drive. Will you take the wheel?" asked Mr Toppol. "Arthur was a fine first-time driver, but I am worried my car might have another disagreement with yet more masonry."

"Aye son, I'll drive. I've got a full clean licence, so

stop worrying and trust me," said the old man as he got into the driver's seat. Mr Toppol smiled with relief and got into the passenger side.

"Well, I did have a full clean licence until they took it off me. Used to have a car too, long time back, until I wrote the bugger off." Mel chuckled. "Hey Arthur, remember that time I thought some swine had stolen my steering wheel and dashboard?"

"Yeah, Mel. I had to point out that you'd actually got into the back seat by mistake."

They all laughed at this. Apart from Mr Toppol, whose tiny bit of confidence in Mel's driving ability disappeared under a cloud of exhaust smoke from a roaringly over-revved engine.

As they mounted kerbs and drove over round-abouts and through red lights, a thought struck Arthur. He leant forward to talk to Mr Toppol who was watching Mel's every grating gear-change with alarm.

"Lesta, what did you mean when you said, *'This has gone far enough.'* You know, in the Underground? And what were you reaching for in your pocket?"

"I simply meant it was time to get some real evidence and show it to the police. I had my mobile which has a digital camera facility with me, but I must have lost it in the struggle."

"Hmmm. Fair enough." Arthur sat back and pondered this. He kept hearing the last words Gwen had said to him. *I love him.* They still caused a pain in his chest each time he remembered them. He took some small comfort from Mel's comical driving and the obvious damage he was doing to Mr Toppol's car.

They arrived back at the school and as before they parked the car where it couldn't be seen from the road.

It was nearly five o'clock, and because it was Saturday it was the Twilight Zone of the weekend. Most people vanish for an hour at this time come a Saturday. Single adults are in putting on their brand new clothes and preening themselves for a night on the town. Married adults are getting tea out of the way so they can sit in front of the telly and complain about how they no longer get out on a Saturday night, or get any brand new clothes. As for kids, they're wrapping up games of football or coming home from a hard day's hanging round a shopping centre. They too like to disappear at this time to have a bite to eat before coming back out again to wander round in gangs wishing away their youth until they too can go out on a Saturday night, get sloshed and vomit on their brand new clothes.*

The two kids, the young teacher and the wrinklies entered the boiler room and looked hesitantly down the hole where the ladder was still in place.

"It seems quiet enough," said Arthur.

* Listen kids, when you're old enough to go boozing on a Saturday night please please please don't throw up on your new clothes like so many other young people. It's not nice. Do it in a taxi instead.

115

"Could be a trap," offered Lawrence.

Nodding, Arthur said, "In that case we must gain the upper hand and retain the element of surprise. Proceed in total silence." Then, ignoring his own good sense he slid down the ladder wailing like a madman, fingers crossed that it wasn't a trap.

It wasn't.

Or at least it didn't seem to be.

The five of them were now on Dead Dobbins platform and there wasn't a sign of any cult members.

All was deathly quiet.

Apart from the racket Mel was making. The old man was braying the hell out of the Shuttington's machine trying to get a drink. He occasionally stopped to re-check his pockets for old money.

"Mel, less it, will you!" snapped Lynn. And he did.

"We need to head for the Hub-office. That's where they'll most probably be," said Mr Toppol.

"And how do we do that?" asked Mel.

"According to the story, there are access points at Hobbler's End and Bobby Boutique. Am I right, Lynn?"

"If memory serves, yes," said the old lady.

"Then let us journey on to Hobbler's and take our chances from there. Agreed?"

"Whoa there, teacher boy. Who snuffed it and left a will naming you as leader of this expedition?" said Arthur sarcastically.

"I apologize, Arthur. You are the master detective

in charge of this case, what do you suggest?" said Mr Toppol apologetically.

"I reckon we should journey on to Hobbler's End and see what happens."

"Fine deduction," said Mr Toppol, patting Arthur's back.

And so they journeyed on with Arthur in charge. Progress was much easier than before as they could now walk between the two metal tracks. Arthur had cleverly deduced that the tracks weren't on. Actually, not that cleverly, as he had touched them to find out.

They were soon at Hobbler's End and although the Time Train was still parked there, there was still no sign of any cult members. Hobbler's was very similar to the other station platforms they had seen. The adverts, the ticket machine and the bricked-up public entrance. But this platform was different insomuch as it had another passageway with a set of steps in it leading down. A sign above them read "Staff Only" and to the side of it was a gate made from small metal criss-crossing rods so it could open and close concertina-style. It was presently open.

They gingerly crept down and the steps stopped below the level of the track. Going directly under the track was another, smaller tunnel – more a walk-way – which was an underpass to the Hub-office. At the end of the tunnel were some more steps, this time leading up to that very room. Mr Toppol stepped in front of Arthur at the bottom of the stairs.

"Wait. I should go first and assess the situation. God alone knows what madness awaits us in the Hub-office," he said, his voice audibly shaky.

"No, I should go first. Gwen, for all her posturing and put-downs, is after all my responsibility," said Arthur nobly.

"Arthur, you are brave beyond your years. If every man in England were you we would still retain our Empire." Mr Toppol placed his hand on Arthur's shoulder.

"Plus if I save her life again I may be on for a bit of a snog and a feel up," said Arthur. "Chicks get really emotional at times like that."

The smile slowly faded from Mr Toppol's face and he turned and ascended the stairs and out of view.

A moment passed and nothing.

Not a sound.

Then bedlam!

Gunshots, shouting, a female scream, much kerfuffle.

"This is it, chaps. Over the top!" cried Arthur. He led the way and they all ran up the stairs and into the Hub-office.

Except it was nothing like an office. It was huge. A large circular room at least 150 metres across. Like the tunnel, it was immaculately tiled and lit with Victorian-style lamps. Around the circumference of the room were occasional closed brass shutters which masked the glass windows that looked out on to each of the six platforms. Far across the room was another entrance the same as the one they had just come through, the doorway leading to Bobby Boutique Station. In the centre of the room was what appeared to be a colossal, brass-plated grandfather clock seven or eight metres high, touching the centre of the domed ceiling. It hummed and resonated with electrical energy. Like the train, it was brass-plated and elaborately adorned in the Victorian style. It had a huge clock face which, wrongly, showed the time as being twenty-five to midnight. The lower part of its large squat body was made up of small pigeonholes, hundreds and hundreds of them, each one containing a battery cell from the passenger carriages of the Time Train. Its upper body was a circular bank of switches, meters, levers and knobs.

More distressing to behold were the people in the Hub-office. The four heroes gasped to see about twenty of the small hooded figures kneeling, praying to the clock.

Arthur scanned the room for Gwen but could not see her. The larger hooded figure from earlier stood facing them, in front of the grandfather clock. He held his gun to the back of Mr Toppol's head, who was kneeling down and looking quite petrified.

"Please, Arthur. Approach with caution. This man is desperate."

"I don't care how much he needs the bog, Toppol. Where is my Gwen? Damn you, sir if you're not the worst kind of lunatic. I charge you now to take your damnable toy train back with you to your own time where you may proceed to drive it up your own tunnel until you both disappear for ever. Show your face you insufferable coward, so I might smash the wretched thing in. Now, damn you!" roared Arthur, his voice quivering slightly.

The hooded figure clicked his fingers and one of the smaller cult members stood and took the gun from him, keeping it trained on Mr Toppol. He then loosened his robe and let it fall to the floor. Underneath he was wearing clothes from more than a century before. A frock coat and Gentlemen's Test-Me-Not-Trousers. But it wasn't so much the garb that made them gasp, it was who was inside them. Arthur and the other good guys could have been knocked down with a proverbial feather because it was not the face of Elle Toppol who looked menacingly at them. It was worse than that. It was the face of. . .

CHAPTER
ELEVEN

B arry Guthries.*

---

* He's the baddie from the first book, The Legend of Arthur King. Have you read
  it? Good, isn't it?

CHAPTER TWELVE

"Guthries!" gasped Arthur. "*You've* been fanny-ing around with the Time Train? No way! No way on this planet," laughed Arthur nervously. "You couldn't work a train set, let alone one that can achieve time travel. You're thicker than a Frenchwoman's facial hair!"

Guthries took back the gun and coolly said, "Two things to bear in mind, Arthur. One, I'm holding a gun. And two, I jumped bail so I could secretly return to Thornaby to kill you."

"Guthries, I've kicked your backside once. Don't make me humiliate you again."

Bang!

The shot echoed loudly around the room, causing Mel, Lynn, Lawrence and Mr Toppol to wince. Arthur fell over as the slug tore across the side of his leg and ricocheted around the room. He squirmed on the tiled floor grasping the gash across his leg, blood oozing from it.

"That's just a little 'a pair of teeth' for what's to come, Arthur," said Guthries coldly.

"It's aperitif, you buffoon festooned with idiocy," said Arthur, desperate to hide his pain.

"You maniac! You shot him!" barked Mel, angrily stepping forward. "Give me that gun, lad, or so help me I'll make you wear it round your flaming neck!"

"Oh lummy, he's angry. I'd better do as he says," said Guthries sarcastically. "Shut up you old fool or I'll put a stop to your pension here and now."

"Where's my sister, Guthries?" shouted Lawrence, stepping forward. Lynn pulled him back.

"Oh she's fine." Guthries turned to the cult members. "Typify." They robotically stood up and rolled off their gowns in unison. This was another eye-opener because they were not the disfigured Morlock/mole people Lawrence and Arthur expected.

It was worse.

They were their fellow pupils. All of them were kids from the Bassleton School of varying ages, and all members of the science club. Lawrence saw two boys from his form class, several other first years, a few second, third and fourth years, and two fifth-year girls. Fay Morgan was one and the other was Gwen! They stood in a neat line, each staring into space as though hypnotized. No expressions. Like supermodels who've just been asked something other than their name.

"What have you done to her, Guthries? Whatever it is, undo it or by God you'll regret it," snarled

123

Arthur as he shakily stood up.

"Thanks for the threat, Arthur, but I don't need any more reason to kill you. I didn't actually re-programme these kids. That was a very clever gentleman from a long time ago called Elle Toppol."

"Where is he?" Arthur looked around the room. He bellowed, "Show yourself, you monster! Show yourself!"

"Here I am, Arthur," said Mr Toppol, suddenly smiling in an oh-so-sinister way.

He stood up.

Lawrence, Mel and Lynn were back in the old "feather/knock down" situation again. Arthur was, by stark contrast, elated.

"Yes!" he cried triumphantly. "I was right all along, you are the baddie!"

Mr Toppol bowed theatrically.

"You?" said Lawrence. "You've been impersonating your great-great-grandfather. Carrying on his work." Lawrence spoke determinedly, but his mind was on something else. He stepped away from Lynn and drew parallel to Guthries, eyeing the gun carefully. At the right moment he would make a swift grab for it.

"You're wrong and you're right, Lawrence. Right that I have been carrying on the great Elle Toppol's work, but no I have not been impersonating him. You see I *am* him. I have indeed travelled nearly a hundred years into my own future. Your present."

This, ordinarily, would be a lot to take in, but after

the events of late it somehow made perfect sense. Well, to most of them.

"I'm confused," said Mel. "More so than normal, actually. Lynn dug a bullet out of you. Who shot you?"

"Guthries did, on my orders. I needed to perpetuate my deceit. You see, when I remarked earlier today, Arthur, that things had gone far enough, I wasn't reaching for a camera. You were right to be suspicious, I was reaching for a gun. It was then that the fair Gwen mentioned Mel and Lynn. I couldn't take the chance there were other witnesses to the Underground running about up there. I had to get you all down here together."

"Yes, well, it's all over now, you madman. Undo whatever it is you've done to my Gwen."

"*Your* Gwen? I think perhaps you're mistaken, Arthur." Mr Toppol smiled cockily, put his arm round Gwen and licked her face. She didn't flinch, she just gazed into space, oblivious to everything.

"Oh God, I am sooooooo going to kick your teeth in for that," said Arthur slowly, so angry he could hardly breathe.

"All my minions from the science club belong to me. All it took was a brief jolt from the Ineffectualator and they were mine. It's a complicated theorem, but to put it very simply I zapped each of them in an area of the brain that deals with logic. Scrambling it. Then I planted a series of trigger words in each of their subconsciouses by whispering

125

to them. Then I gave each one sealed orders which they read and later destroyed. All I needed to do then was utter the trigger words again and – hussars! – they'd be totally under my control."

"Well that stands to reason. You'd never get anyone barmy enough to follow you of their own accord. You're a raving bonkers idiot who wants locking up," said Mel. "So there."

"Oh I am locked up, Mel. We all are. Trapped in a twenty-first century nightmare prison of technology where science is even more of a jailer than it was in my own time. Even your peasants have computers and cars, like that thug I showed you in the science club. The lower classes shouldn't have access to computers and mobiles and God knows what else. What the hell's gone wrong with the order of society in my near century of absence?"

"Things have got better and thankfully there's hardly any stuck up prats like you around any more," shouted Mel.

Ignoring him*, Toppol continued, "You've all grown so soft with your little luxuries. Your cable-TV, DVDs, microwave ovens. It's monstrous how happy you are to be such slaves to electricity! Take away electricity and the lower classes would starve to death. They haven't the intelligence to even open a tin of beans for themselves. That's the beauty of my plan, you see. In the Stone Age, only the

* Mel was obviously of working class origins so whatever he had to say wasn't worth hearing.

intelligent and resourceful will survive. The fat, bloated wasters of this world will wither and die. I'm separating the wheat from the chaff. We will rise from being mere Homo sapiens to being Homo superiors.*"

Arthur sneered at Toppol and said, "You're ranting, man. We have a society built on equality where no man is bigger and better than the other. Where you don't have to be mega-rich or mega-intelligent to have a say." He paused. "Obviously there's still scum like Guthries around, but on the whole we're quite a happy little country."

Guthries sneered at Arthur and turned the gun on him to stick a slug in the other leg. Lawrence took his cue. He jumped forward, slammed his fist in Guthries's face and grabbed the gun. He trained it on Toppol.

"Don't move or he gets it!" he said seriously. Then he smiled. "Ha, I've always wanted to say something like that."

"Good work, Lawrence!" laughed Arthur. "Do us a favour and stick a couple of slugs in Guthries, will you, mate?"

"To slow him down a bit?" asked Lawrence, aiming the gun at Guthries.

"Well I didn't actually have a reason, but I can live with that," answered Arthur.

"Lawrence, you do realize you too were zapped by

---

* A gay joke occurred to Mel but he decided to leave it for the time being.

127

my Ineffectualator," said Mr Toppol cockily.

Lawrence gasped with the realization.

"Oh cack!" he said. "Arthur, quick take the gun!"

It was too late. Mr Toppol spoke the word.

"Abramelin."

In an instant Lawrence's expression faded to nothing and he handed the gun to Mr Toppol and took his place with the other cult members. Arthur, Mel and Lynn sighed.

"Oh very well, Toppol, give us the big dire plan bit before you kill us," said Arthur nonchalantly. "Isn't it baddie law you have to, or something."

"Then I shall not fly in the face of tradition, Arthur," said Mr Toppol, smiling. "I am Lesta Toppol. There is a coffin full of soil buried in Thornaby cemetery. The people of my time believed the coffin contained me. A fortunate spelling mistake on my gravestone has aided me in my deceit. Instead of saying L Toppol, those idiot stonemasons carved Elle Toppol. It was of great help to me once I came to this era and needed a *nom-de-plume*."

Mel went to speak, but Mr Toppol anticipated him.

"An alternative name, Mel." The old fellow nodded. "As far as the people of this time know, Elle Toppol is dead and I, Lesta Toppol, am his innocent descendant."

"Come on, Toppol, no more talk. Give me Arthur and I can be about my business," demanded Guthries. He sneered at Arthur. "I'm going to kill you. You are actually going to die. How do you feel about that?"

Arthur shrugged his shoulders and said, "I'm 13. I've had a good innings."

This infuriated Guthries and he slapped Arthur's face.

"Patience, Barry. All things come to he who waits," said Mr Toppol.

"A marriage made in hell this, isn't it?" asked Arthur, pointing to Guthries and Toppol. "How did such a lovely couple like you meet?"

"When I emerged from the Underground, just after my train pulled into this century, I clawed my way out of the service duct in the ceiling and found Barry here hiding out in the old wood warehouse. He was living rough whilst plotting your death, Arthur. We just hit it off. Barry's been assisting me with the refuelling of the grandfather clock. Each trip we make across the leylines refills the temporal energy in the cells and I now have enough power to complete my plan."

"Yes, you have," said Barry, smiling wickedly. "You don't need me no more. I can take Arthur away somewhere and play with him. Am I right?"

"Half right, Barry. Insomuch as I don't need you any more."

Toppol trained the gun on Barry and fired.

Blam!

Guthries was dead before he hit the floor.

CHAPTER THIRTEEN

Lynn screamed. Mel gasped.

Arthur, so shocked at seeing someone die in front of him, even Guthries, fell to his knees and threw up.

"You psycho! He's dead!" snarled Mel.

"Oh I'm hardly that. I'm just a tad eccentric. Besides, it's only Guthries. Where we're all going there won't be any shortage of cavemen. One less won't matter."

"You're really going to do it! You're going to try and send us all back in time, to start from scratch in the Stone Age?" gasped Mel.

"Of course. Which do you fancy – the Palaeolithic, the Mesolithic or the Neolithic?"

"Oooh, surprise us," said Arthur in his most fierce and sarcastic tone.

Mr Toppol didn't like the remark, but ignored it. "I tried in 1908 but it failed. Miscalculations and faulty circuitry, to put it simply. I ended up nearly a century in the future." He turned to the grandfather clock and stroked it lovingly. "This old fellow is so temperamental. Aren't you, sir? You see it's this device that controls both the Global Field Emitter and the Temporal Energy Drive. I won't bore you with the details, no time really, but the Global Field is a wave of energy that encompasses every living creature on this planet in an instant, at the speed of time to be precise. Nothing without a human aura is affected. I only want to take back man and animal-kind. Buildings, cars, and more importantly, weapons and technology, will be left behind here in the present. Then and only then can we start afresh."

"How come your daft train came through time then? That's not alive," asked Arthur.

"When the correct speed is achieved it passes right out of this dimension rendering it free to travel anywhere. I need the train to create the Earth energy spark. Think of the power in this grandfather clock as the petrol-soaked kindling and the train as the match. The catalyst. But this time the Global Field will not collapse as it did in 1908."

"That's what went wrong the first time, and threw you forward to our time?" asked Lynn.

"Yes. The field funnelled into a beam of un-imaginably intense energy. It hit and levelled an area of Siberia called Tunguska. But now I have perfected my apparatus it cannot fail again." He rolled his eyes and gave a boyish smile. "Fingers crossed."

"You're insane, Toppol! Insane!" roared Arthur, making a swipe at the gun. The pain in his leg was getting worse and he fell to the floor as Toppol stepped back.

"Yes, but you'll all thank me for it one day."

"What about medicines? Technology has cured many ailments and diseases," pleaded Lynn. "If you whisk us all back to the Stone Age what will ill people do?"

"Erm, die probably. It'll be survival of the fittest. We'll emerge a stronger, purer breed of human." He smiled again. "Now I think we're done here." He looked up at the clock face towering above them. It said five to twelve. "Ah yes, bang on schedule. At the stroke of midnight I shall release the 'spark', so to speak, from inside my train and we shall step out into a new day long long ago."

"What about us?" asked Arthur, looking down at Guthries's dead body. "Are we going the same way he did?"

"Shut up," whispered Mel frantically. "Don't give him ideas."

"Goodness me, no, Arthur. I really admire you. You have brains and guts. That's why I liquidated Guthries, to save your life. We'll need people like you to help build a new utopia in the Stone Age. I am allowing you to live, and the old fogies too as I can see you're quite attached to them. Now to business."

He handed the gun to Fay who trained it on Arthur, Mel and Lynn. He then pressed a couple of buttons on the grandfather clock and two things happened.

Firstly, the brass shutter nearest to them slowly clanked into life and rose to reveal a large glass viewing screen. Out of it the platform of Hobbler's End Station could be seen directly across the track. The Time Train was still parked there.

"Mel and Lynn won't miss the show now," smiled Mr Toppol.

Secondly, a panel on the grandfather clock rose to reveal a brass handle in front of three settings: PAST, PRESENT, FUTURE. It was currently resting on PRESENT. Mr Toppol gently eased the lever to PAST and the grandfather clock instantly hummed and resonated louder and stronger. The power inside was obviously of cataclysmic proportions, just waiting to be set free.

"Sentry," said Mr Toppol, pulling Arthur to one side and taking the gun back from Fay. Immediately the cult members formed a circle around Mel and Lynn, closing in tightly like sardines in a tin. Mel tried to prise them apart but they were solid, each jamming hard against the other. There was no way out.

Mr Toppol ruffled Arthur's hair playfully.

"Now. Who wants to come for a ride in my big shiny Time Train?"

"Get stuffed," said Arthur.

"Well you're coming anyway, so I can keep my eye on you."

He pushed the gun into Arthur's back and frog-marched him out of the room via the passageway to Hobbler's End.

CHAPTER
FOURTEEN

They emerged on to the platform. Arthur looked directly across the tracks and could see into the Hub-office. Mel and Lynn were desperately trying to prise the kids apart, but to no avail. They walked towards the waiting train.

"I faked my own death in 1908 in case the big show failed. Which it did. I thought, then, I would be free to recharge the train and keep trying until it did work. Remember what I said about always thinking ahead. I vowed to myself that I wouldn't leave the Underground until I had perfected the time travel technique. However, after the train slowed down I sensed something was wrong, but I couldn't work out what. It was only when I climbed up through the secret hatch into the wood warehouse that I found I was 97 years in the future. The tunnel is scientifically sealed so it had lain untouched by human or vermin hand. It hadn't aged in all that time. Interesting, eh?"

"Paws," said Arthur blankly and Mr Toppol stopped walking for a second and dropped his gun-hand to his side. Arthur turned to him and said, "Not pause, paws. Vermin have paws not hands."

"Ah, right, I get you."

They carried on walking to the train and Arthur realized he had just missed a golden opportunity to do something. "Damn," he said to himself.

Mr Toppol opened the door to the driver's carriage and pushed Arthur in.

"Anyway, once I got out and befriended my young chum, Barry—"

"Whom you've just shot dead," interrupted Arthur.

"The very same. Shame, that."

"Oh, so you do have some remorse then."

"No, shame I ruined that suit of mine. I loaned it to Barry to try and spruce him up a bit, but it didn't work. You can't polish dung. Anyway, where was I? Oh yes. Well it was plain sailing after that. Lied my way into a teaching job. Barry kept the aircraft hangar guarded, until he had to torch it of course, and oversaw the work programmes I had instilled into the minds of the science club members. That's why I started the club – to seek out inquisitive young minds. They're the best for handling the intricacies of my quantum machinery. They've been like my little bee-drones nurturing my little honey pots of golden energy."

"You are so insane, Toppol," remarked Arthur.

"Obviously it's only a temporary state of hypnosis. That was an essential part of the plan. When we

135

emerge into the new Stone Age I couldn't possibly allow anyone but myself to have knowledge like that. It has to remain a one-way trip. I have instilled a memory delete mechanism in each of them. A simple trigger word and they'll snap out of their hypnosis and forget everything I've taught them. Even the memory of the Underground. You can be in charge of that if you like. The word is *Lethean*. In Greek mythology there was a river in Hades called Lethe which caused forgetfulness if you drank from it. But you knew that, didn't you."

"Of course," lied Arthur.

"Say that and they'll be right as rain. Regretful. I rather enjoyed having my own little faction of guardian angels. It was quite nice."

"It's quite barking, actually," corrected Arthur.

"Arthur, your quips are not appreciated. You should be honoured. You will actually be witness to the greatest scientific breakthrough in history! You'll be able to tell your kids you were actually present when Lesta Toppol split the second. Oppenheimer and co splitting little atoms to release energy was just peanuts compared to this. This is the big one."

Arthur watched him dextrously manipulate the controls on the dashboard. Pushing this knob, flicking that switch, setting that dial. He pulled a lever to a down position and instantly the tracks gave a powerful *zooooz*-type sound as if to say, "We're ready!"

He eased forward the accelerator handle Arthur

had used on their first visit to the Underground, and the train set off jerklessly.

"Toppol, listen to me. You don't have to do this. Why not use your insane evil genius for good?" said Arthur, trying to reason with him. "You could be the richest man alive with your knowhow."

"I practically was, a century ago, but it didn't make me happy. Besides, we won't need money where we're going, Arthur. No need for it. There won't anything to buy. No businesses, no houses and definitely no shops."

"I'll bet there'll still be a McDonald's somewhere," quipped Arthur glumly.

"Wouldn't surprise me, Arthur," laughed Toppol as he increased the train's velocity.

"Toppol. Mr Toppol. Lesta, listen. You don't have the right to do this! You are not the judge, jury and executioner for mankind!"

"Arthur, Arthur, Arthur. You're not seeing the bigger picture here. Look at what the world is. It's a shambolic mess. Crime is rife. Kids on drugs. Old people mugged. The wrong kind of people having a say has led to all these little wars going on around the planet. There's a million madmen out there trying to blow up another million madmen, and what's behind it all? Technology. We've come too far, too soon. I'm actually saving the world from itself. A new start. Point zero. Back to the old drawing board and this time, with any luck, we'll get it right."

"Isn't it a bit ironic you've created the most

intricate and phenomenal piece of technological hardware in the history of the world and you want to use it to end all technology?" reasoned Arthur, frantically looking around for something big and heavy to cosh the mad sod with.

"Yes. The greatest irony of them all. Once the deed is done I shall dismantle the machine and never again shall I look upon a schematic diagram. That I swear. I'm going to grow vegetables, me. What will you do? You'll need to do something. There'll be no telly back then."

"And no Thornaby Underground!" said Arthur sharply. "Aha! You didn't think of that, did you? This thing might appear in some Stone Age rock mountain."

"Nope. The Manifest-Compensators ensure that can't happen. They'll find us a clear area to appear in."

"Then, what about causality? Huh? What effect will the entire population of the twenty-first century have on the population of evolving humans and animals of the Stone Age?"

"Catastrophic, with any luck. The creatures of that time will have to be systematically wiped out, lest they might evolve into what mankind is now. We're not making the same mistake twice."

"OK then, what about time paradox theories? They are our ancestors. If they die, we die. We will vanish from history."

"Nope, you're wrong. We'll be in a set timeline. Think of it like this. If we sent a bomb back to the

Stone Age and set it off by remote control, thus wiping out all life on earth, yes, then we'd vanish from history. But, because we're actually taking everyone back to that previous time we'll become part of that timeline. It's easy really."

By now Arthur had lost all hope of getting through to Toppol. Then he spied something that might be able to help him, or at least buy him some time. Across the windows he saw the crushed velvet curtains hanging from the thick brass rods. Slowly reaching up, Arthur took hold of one.

"Thank goodness for Victorian decadence," he said to himself.

* * *

Back in the Hub-office, Mel and Lynn tried in vain to get free from the compacted fence of hypnotized kids encircling them.

"The human body must be much more powerful with a concentrated mind," said Lynn. "There's no way these kids could compress so tightly otherwise."

"That helps," said Mel sarcastically.

"I'm just pointing it out, that's all."

"Tell it to the dinosaur we'll be meeting in a few minutes' time," snapped Mel.

"Don't get clever with me, Melvyn Havilland," she retorted. "And dinosaurs pre-date the Stone Age anyway."

"Spare me the history lesson, pet, I'll see it all first hand unless we can shift these ruddy brats."

* * *

Very carefully, very slowly, while Toppol checked every dial and readout on the dashboard, Arthur took down the curtain pole.

"Toppol, that grandfather clock – I noticed it had past *and* future settings. Why send us to the past? Why not the future? Perhaps one day we will evolve into a civilized race of intellectuals living in a peaceful utopia."

"Nah, that's just science-fiction silliness."

Arthur shook his head and looked around the Time Train and for once, just briefly, realized what irony was.

"It's all silliness and it ends here, I'm afraid, mush."

Mr Toppol turned to look at him just as Arthur brought down the end of the heavy brass curtain pole on his head, knocking the loon to the floor and out cold.* Arthur moved the accelerator back to zero and the train slowed sufficiently for him to gauge a full stop at Hobbler's End. He bound Toppol's arms and legs with the curtain ties and limped back to the Hub-office.

* Oooh, so you can knock someone out with one blow. I stand corrected.

CHAPTER
FIFTEEN

Arthur, what happened to Toppol?" gasped Mel with glee as the lad entered the room.

"Let's just say it was curtains for Mr Toppol." He looked at the cult members, frozen like statues.

"Can you free us, Arthur?" asked Lynn.

"Yes. That idiot Toppol made the fatal mistake of telling me the trigger word to bring them round. What an absolute jerk," Arthur laughed.

There was a long pause, punctuated by Arthur shaking his head and making mocking noises about Toppol.

"Say it then," said Lynn expectantly.

"I've forgotten it for the moment." Arthur bit his lip and thought hard. "I know." He turned to the cult members. "Your master, Mr Toppol, is in grave danger. He needs you."

Led by Gwen, the zombie-like kids filed out in search of their leader.

"Smart thinking, Arthur," said Lynn, "Come on, we need to fetch the law."

"No, there's no time. I have to disengage this machine somehow." They stepped over to the grandfather clock and walked round it, examining every aspect of it.

"There's a little map of the world here all lit up?" said Mel, pointing to a little map of the world which was all lit up. The centre of it was the north of England and, in circles pushing outwards, the entire globe was illuminated.

"This must be something to do with the Global What-not Field," said Arthur, frantically trying to find an "off" switch. "How do you disengage the rotten thing?"

Lynn had the answer, she had taken off her shoe and slammed the heel down on the glass map, cracking it. The machinery inside must have been delicate indeed because it sparked and creaked and stopped working. The circular lights went out one by one, like a ripple effect in reverse, until none were lit.

"Well, that's done it," said Mel, nodding at Lynn. "Sorted."

"No, no, no, Mel. I don't understand all this, but he still has the power of time travel, the power in this grandfather clock," remarked Arthur.

"Well let's smash that then," said Mel, lifting his leg and booting the side of the clock.

"Good God, no!" screamed Lynn. "That would be like blowing up the electricity board to turn off a light. The power in this is immeasurable, it has to go somewhere. Let it all out now and there'll be so many Rips in the fabric of time every age will meld into one. It'd be the end of time as we know it."

"She's right. We'll use the power as it was intended, but send the train alone back in time. Where it can do no more harm. Come on."

They began rushing out to do just that.

"You're dead sexy when you talk quantum mechanics, Lynn," whispered Mel. She threw him a wink.

They emerged back on to Hobbler's End platform and a sudden pang of panic hit Arthur. What would they find there?

They soon found out.

The twenty kids were stood in a line behind the now unbound Mr Toppol who had that terrible look all teachers display when they know they've caught you doing something you shouldn't have, red-handed! Plus, this teacher had a ruddy gun!

"Drat," said Arthur. "I should have maybe thought this out a little better."

"Arthur," said Mr Toppol sternly, "you really are testing my patience." He pulled the criss-cross metal gate shut and locked it, pocketing the key. "I really wanted you to work with me on this project. But oh no, you have to play the decent Englishman and do what's right. I'm sorry Arthur, there's no place for troublemakers in my Stone Age paradise. I'm going to shoot you dead."

Arthur winced and tensed up, but Toppol didn't

pull the trigger. He stopped and thought for a moment.

"I have a more rounded idea. I won't shoot you."

Arthur sighed with relief.

"Gwen can do it." He handed the gun to Gwen and said, "Gwen, I order you to execute Arthur when I say the word."

Without hesitation Gwen took the gun and put the barrel against Arthur's forehead.

Lynn screamed.

Mel froze.

Arthur tried to think what the trigger word was so he could bring Gwen and all the others round. But he still couldn't remember it!

"Leap something. Leave. No, leeks, no that's stupid. Erm, Leave, no I've tried that! Oh cobblers."

"I'm sorry, Arthur, I really have to take your first answer. You gambled, you lost. Now here's your booby prize," said Toppol. "Gwen, fire."

"Gwen, I can see up your skirt!" he shouted, his eyes wide with fear.

A flicker of hesitation passed over her face.

"What are you doing, Arthur?" asked Lynn.

"Female psychology! There's nothing a girl hates more than being ogled by someone she doesn't fancy! If I can fill her head with that thought it may block out Toppol's hypnosis thingy."

Gwen was slowly lowering the gun.

"Gwen, do as I instructed and kill Arthur," snapped Toppol. "Stop being inventive, Arthur, and die!"

Gwen put the barrel back to Arthur's head.

"I bet you've got that lacy white bra on today. Or-or-or the shiny black one. H-h-have you? That's my favourite!" Arthur felt light-headed with fear. Gwen flopped her arm down and looked as if she was awakening from a very bad dream.

"Amazing," said Lynn. "Who'd have thought your perverted ogling would one day save your life."

Mr Toppol checked his watch. "You're really getting on my wick now, boy! Your meddling has made me late for a very important date. And for that alone, Arthur, I shall shoot you myself," he said, reaching for the gun.

"Oh no you won't!" It was Mel. He ran at Toppol and head-butted the side of his face. The teacher fell against the tiled wall and on to the floor.

"Christ, I'm going to have a headache tomorrow," said Mel, rubbing his forehead and taking the gun off Gwen. She staggered and Arthur supported her.

"Wh-where am I?" she asked. She rubbed her eyes and looked at Arthur. "Er, get off me you dirty little creep." She slapped Arthur round the face.

He smiled widely. "That's the Gwen I know!" he said.

"It looks like it's all over, Toppol," said Mel with a cocky smile. "And it's about time. Ha!" Mel thought that was a really clever thing to say. So did Lynn and gave him an approving nod.

"Where's he gone?" asked Arthur with alarm.

Mr Toppol wasn't on the floor where he had

fallen. There was a *shunt* noise and they all turned to see him locking the cabin door of the driver's engine from the inside.

"I'll see you in the Stone Age!" he shouted.

Arthur ran to the door and tried to force it open. In the cabin Toppol was re-aligning his equipment.

"Toppol, it's over! We smashed the Global Beam thing. If you go back, you'll go alone! I've ruined all your plans!"

Toppol's face contorted with blind fury and he punched the window hard, splitting his knuckles.

"You idiot! You've ruined all my plans!"

"I know, I just said that."

Toppol snorted like a bull, thinking hard. His eyes lit up.

"You haven't done anything, Arthur. Nothing at all."

"I have. Like I said, the Global beam thing is knackered and—"

Toppol interrupted him. "In this timeline, yes. I'll simply go back two days and kill the Arthur of that time. The grandfather clock is set on PAST, and there's no way back into the Hub-office. I locked the gate, remember! Ha!"

"Oooh, you sneaky little man!" said Lynn.

"I'll change the recent past and my plans will be back on track. See you later, Arthur. Or should that be *earlier*."

He reached for the accelerator handle and pushed it forward. The train shot off at speed, whizzing out of sight.

For a moment no one knew what to say.

"He can't really do that, can he?" asked Mel.

"Yes, he can," sighed Lynn.

"Balls," said Arthur.

Woooooooooosh! The train had done the full circle and shot past again, gathering in momentum.

Wooooooosh! It passed again.

A pause.

Wooooosh! It passed again.

A shorter pause.

Woosh! It passed again.

Soon there was only a few seconds between passes as the train roared past again and again and again. It would be less than a minute before it reached its optimum time-travelling speed and would fade from this dimension.

Out of reach.

And the Arthur King of two days ago would be dead.

CHAPTER
SIXTEEN

But the Arthur of now wasn't finished yet. He had an idea.

"Mel, pass me the gun," he said sharply.

Mel handed him it and said, "Come on Arthur, a little bullet hitting a train at that speed isn't going to stop it."

"I'm not aiming for the train."

Arthur pointed the gun at the glass window of the Hub-office, timed the passing of the Train in his head, and fired.

Blam!

Crash!

The window disintegrated into millions of tiny pieces. Arthur walked towards the edge of the platform, turned his back on the track and stepped over to the bricked-up entrance. Seven steps he counted in his head. He turned again and faced the track, standing directly in front of the shattered window of the Hub-office.

Wooosh! went the train on another pass.

"Now what?" asked Mel. Lynn had twigged what

he was about to try. It was futile, surely. Perhaps, but she knew Arthur could not be talked out of it and he had nothing to lose.

Counting out loud and timing the passing of the train, Arthur ran forward as fast as he could and leapt off the edge of the platform.

Into the air above the track he flew.

Into the open window frame of the Hub-office.

He made it.

But only just.

His timing was flawed.

The speeding train clipped his ankle most severely. Arthur was sent spinning on to the tiled floor, making a sound like a wet fish being dropped from a ten-storey building. He spun round and round and round coming to a stop in front of the grandfather clock.

He was dazed and silent for a second.

Then he screamed at the pain in his ankle, tears running down his face. He felt cold and sick inside, but he knew what he had to do. Digging his nails against the ridges in the tiles he pulled himself forward in the direction of the grandfather clock. He grunted and groaned and seethed to himself, angry that the pain was almost unbearable. He reached the clock and pulled himself up level with the brass handle which was set at PAST. He gripped it and with all his might he pushed it to FUTURE. Then beyond that mark, off the scale so the metal buckled and jammed. Sparks shot out from the grandfather clock and the once unfaultable sound of its inner mechanisms became that of offset whirrings and grating, grinding clunks.

* * *

Inside the Time Train Lesta Toppol was ready to make the leap into Temporal Drive. He was furious and elated at the same time. Angry at having his plans scuppered by a boy, but elated that he had found a way round the problem.

He would go back two days in time, kill Arthur and help the Lesta Toppol of that time to complete the plan. Yes, it would work so much better with two Lesta Toppols in charge. "Fantastic," he said to himself.

Oh how wrong he was.

He didn't know it yet, but Lesta Toppol wasn't going a few days into the past. He was off on a journey in another direction. He held the switch which operated the Temporal Drive and flicked it to ON and the Time Train evaporated from the early twenty-first century like hot steam in a cold whirlwind.

* * *

On Hobbler's End station the cult members were stood stock-still, gazing into space, awaiting orders from their leader. Orders that would never come. Mel and Lynn, who were comforting the dazed Gwen, gasped as the Time Train vanished on its final pass. There was suddenly total silence in the tunnel. Not a single sound. It seemed to go on for ever before finally being broken by a voice from across the tracks.

It was Arthur.

"Can someone give me a hand? My ankle's really knacking me."

"Did you do it?" asked Lynn with terrified anticipation.

"I'm still here, aren't I? Of course I did it!"

Lynn leapt for joy.

Behind him, Arthur heard a crackle and a fizz. He spun round and to his horror saw a gash in the very air appear. He blinked and gasped. This was the first time he'd actually witnessed a Time Rip. It undulated and opened wider.

Hobbling over to it, Arthur peered into it. He saw a scene from around twenty minutes ago. He saw himself, Mel and Lynn talking to Toppol and the cult members stood in a line.

"This just happened, surely?" he said to himself.

Walking around the Rip he gasped when he saw that Barry Guthries was there too, a pre-murder Barry Guthries who was standing up, as opposed to the very dead one on the floor in the present. Arthur remembered that this was just seconds before Toppol shot Guthries dead. Arthur's mind began to reel with possibilities.

Could he? Should he?

Did Guthries deserve a helping hand?

151

"Come on, Toppol, no more talk. Give me Arthur and I can be about my business," demanded Guthries. He sneered at Arthur, "I'm going to kill you. You are actually going to die. How do you feel about that?"

Arthur shrugged his shoulders and said, "I'm 13. I've had a good innings."

This infuriated Guthries and he slapped Arthur's face.

"Patience, Barry. All things come to he who waits," said Mr Toppol.

"A marriage made in hell this, isn't it?" asked Arthur pointing to Guthries and Toppol. "How did such a lovely couple like you meet?"

"When I emerged from the Underground, just after my train pulled into this century, I clawed my way out of the service duct in the ceiling and found Barry here hiding out in the old wood warehouse. He was living rough whilst plotting your death, Arthur. We just hit it off. Barry's been assisting me with the refuelling of the grandfather clock. Each trip we make across the leylines refills the temporal energy in the cells and I now have enough power to complete my plan."

"Yes, you have," said Barry, smiling wickedly. "You don't need me no more. I can take Arthur away somewhere and play with him. Am I right?"

"Half right, Barry. Insomuch as I don't need you any more." Toppol trained the gun on Barry and. . .

. . . before he could fire, a hand appeared from out of thin air. It grabbed Barry Guthries by the scruff of his neck and yanked him backwards. In a trice both the arm and Guthries were gone.

Arthur, Mel, Lynn and Mr Toppol paused for a moment.

"Well there's something you don't see every day," said Mr Toppol. "No matter, he was about to be put out of the picture anyway."

* * *

In the Hub-office of the present Arthur wrenched Guthries clear of the Time Rip an instant before it closed. Giddy and disorientated by his short trip through time, Guthries fell to the floor next to his own corpse. He then screamed and rose to his knees. His eyes bulged at the sight of his own dead body, the large bullet hole in its chest and the massive pool of blood under it. His blood!

"Oh my God, I'm dead! I'm dead!" screamed the terrified thug.

And then the corpse twinkled and flickered as the timelines corrected themselves. It vanished out of existence because now, thanks to Arthur, Barry Guthries never died.

Guthries turned to Arthur who was now looking very pleased with himself.

"Did he. . .? Toppol, did he. . .? Am I. . .? Was I. . .? Did he shoot me?"

"Yup. You were deader than a bus driver's personality, mate."

153

"You saved my life? *You* did? Arthur King? The kid I was going to kill?"

"Lordy yes. It was quite fortuitous that you happened to be standing exactly where one of the Time Rips appeared. Created by Toppol's most recent and final trip through time," explained Arthur.

"I owe you my life," said Barry, with genuine emotion.

"Then stop trying to take mine," Arthur shouted, prodding Barry hard in the chest, the exact spot where Mr Toppol had shot him. "Deal?"

"Deal," said Barry.

"Do those kids out there respond to you as well as Toppol?"

"They do, yeah."

"And do you know the trigger word to release them from their hypnosis?"

"Yeah, it's Lethean."

"Oooh, I was so close! Right, get those kids back up the ladder and as far away from here as possible and say the word. Not Lawrence, I need him fully conscious here. Then you get back here, pronto. We have a lot of work to do."

CHAPTER SEVENTEEN

It took them seven hours to do it, but in the grand scheme of time it could have taken them seven years, it wouldn't have mattered. The effects of their toil would not be appreciated for millennia, but they didn't have the exact timetable.

Arthur watched from where he was sitting on Mr Toppol's car bonnet as Guthries struggled past him with another large rock. Into the boiler room he went and dropped it down the hole.

It landed at Hobbler's End station platform with an almighty crash. When it settled, Mel rolled it on to the track where Lawrence, Gwen and Lynn positioned it with the others. By now there was a good-sized pile of rocks, bricks, bits of school fence and the spare wheel from Mr Toppol's car boot.

Guthries stepped out of the boiler room and pointed to the car door leant against the wall, which he and Arthur had previously taken off.

"Now the door, Arthur?" asked Guthries.

"Yeah. But let me do just one last thing, Barry."

Arthur hopped over to it and began scratching

words on it with a screwdriver he found in the glove box. When he had finished Barry chucked it down the hole and Mel shoved it on to the track. Once everyone was out from the Underground Mel screwed down the hatch, sealing the tunnel for good.

"We'll keep hold of Toppol's keys and I'll come back here tomorrow with a bag of cement and re-concrete the floor. Seal it up proper," said the old fellow.

"Good idea, Mel," said Arthur. "There were never any workmen laying pipes in here. Just Toppol slipping in and out of his Underground whenever he pleased. Which is obviously why he chose to teach at this school in the first place." He turned to Guthries. "And what will you be up to now, Guthries?"

"Dunno." The big lad shrugged his shoulders. "Do something. Something good for a change. Seeing my dead body on the Hub-office floor really made me realize how little time we have. It's astounding, Arthur. Seventy years if you're lucky. That's the human lifespan and I've wasted a good chunk of it doing nothing but making decent people miserable. I'm not wasting another second of my life."

"Indubitably, Barry. If only every thug, thief and criminal could be saved from death and set on a course of righteousness by an incursion in the laws of physics, this world would be a far safer place," said Arthur, patting Barry's shoulder.

"If only, eh?" said Barry pulling a face to the

others. And with that the big lad ran off.

"Think Fay and the others really will have no memory of the Underground?" asked Mel.

"Definitely," said Gwen. "I can't remember anything about the Hub-office. At least, not of actually being there, only what you've told me since. It's scary to think that I might have spent every weekend for the last few months down there working on that train and never known what I was doing."

Lawrence added, "And I can't remember a single thing after I snatched the gun from Guthries. Weird city, man." He looked sheepishly at Arthur. "I mean, a most perplexing cerebral state to find oneself in."

"I think the silence of the science club is assured," said Arthur.

"What will Mr Toppol find when he arrives at his destination, Arthur?" asked Gwen.

He looked at the beautiful girl in front of him whom he worshipped so dearly and heard again the words she spoke earlier that day in the tunnel: *I love him.* It didn't hurt so much now. It was probably one of the effects of Toppol's Ineffectualator that made her say that.

He hoped.

"I have no idea, but I know it's very nasty," said Arthur, taking a breath. "Lesta Toppol's dead."

"How could you possibly know that, Arthur? You sent him to the distant future. He could be working with technology beyond our wildest dreams to return to this time and exact his dire revenge on

157

each of us," said Gwen, working it out with alarm.

"Definitely not. Otherwise he'd have done it already. I'd be dead and you lot would be in the Stone Age."

They all stopped and took it in, nodding with their bottom lips stuck out. Lawrence looked both ways as they crossed the deserted street. Not for cars – for cavemen.

* * *

Inside the Time Train Lesta Toppol watched as the Temporal Energy indicator dropped to zero. The power now totally spent. The train suddenly slowed and the distorted time that flashed past the windows began to un-blur and the familiar white tiles of the Thornaby Underground reappeared. He looked out of the windows and the train got slower and slower. The familiar signs of the Underground stations whizzed by.

Boneyard and Bobby Boutique.

Station Station.

Mutznutts.

Dead Dobbins.

Then sheer panic.

He had only seconds to take in the site of a large pile of rocks and other debris placed deliberately on the track. And on top of it was an ancient yet still shiny hunk of metal that had once been a car door, and carved on to it were the words. . .

Then Toppol blacked out as the train crashed into the rocks and his head slammed against the windscreen. The train careered up off the tracks and smashed through the tunnel ceiling. The entire train was crushed in on itself like a thin Coke can and concertinaed into a twisted mangle of metal as it roared still upwards through brittle rock. The screeching of metal slowly dissipated as the train stopped moving, its sole occupant stunned and dazed.

Then he awoke.

A bloody, ripped hand appeared out of the wreckage, followed by the other. A battered, bruised and gory-looking Lesta Toppol mustered what little strength his bashed and broken body had and pulled himself free of the carnage and fell on to something hot.

He blinked the blood out of his eyes and stood up. He saw sunlight. Not the gentle orange sunlight one might have expected. The sun was blood-red and huge. Fifty times bigger than it should have been and unfathomably more powerful.

And then he noticed he was standing on sand.

Hot, burning sand.

He was hallucinating, he thought to himself.

He gagged and choked on the crisp dry air. It throttled the inside of his throat and he fell back to the sand, gasping for breath.

He looked around himself and saw the train had somehow propelled itself up out of the sand and stood up at an angle like some deranged statue. One solitary monument on a bleak desert landscape with absolutely nothing else for as far as the eye could see. Earth's entire surface was now covered in a dense layer of burning sand.

Lesta Toppol would never discover why he wasn't two days in the past. He would never know he was in the future, or how far into the future he was. He'd never uncover what had actually happened to the Earth in his absence . . . for two good reasons.

Firstly, there was no one left to tell him. Everyone had left this dying planet a thousand years ago. Mankind had scattered to the stars and now prospered on a hundred worlds far far away. The sun had gone supernova and had rendered the planet a burning, uninhabitable furnace.

The second reason Lesta Toppol would never know what had happened, and perhaps the most important one, was that in less than twenty more seconds of breathing in the crisp, poisonous air of three thousand years in the future, he would be dead.

And no one would ever hear the final words on his blistering lips.

"Arthur bloody King."

EPILOGUE

Arthur King stood supported by Lawrence as, together with Gwen and Lynn, they watched Mel park Mr Toppol's car on the side of the road opposite the Bassleton School and get out. He ran to join them and the five of them began walking across Thornaby town centre towards home.

"I don't understand," said Gwen. "Surely the police will find the car and trace it back to Mr Toppol. Then they'll do an extensive search for him, including the school, and maybe find the Underground. Why not hide it somewhere it'll never be found?"

"It's called The Old Bike Supposition, Gwen," said Arthur. "If you want rid of anything, absolutely anything, particularly an old bike, all you need do is leave it out in the street and you can guarantee than within minutes someone will nick it. Then it's off your hands for ever."

"It's true," said Mel. "I've got rid of old mattresses, sideboards, sofas, girlfriends, you name it, over the years. It never fails."

"Oh come on, that's just silly, isn't it?" Gwen turned round to look at the car just in time to see it as a speck in the distance being driven off at speed by God knows who.

"Oh, right, cool," said the rare beauty, genuinely impressed.

They walked on a while, discussing the events of the last few days. Soon, despite Arthur's damaged lower extremities slowing their pace too much, they were in Sherwood Road. Mel and Lynn yawned as they said goodnight and went into their house.

"I'll call for you in the morning, Arth," said Lawrence, he too of yawny head. He walked on.

Gwen turned to Arthur and smiled sweetly. "Once again, Arthur King, I owe you a great debt."

"Yes, I suppose so." He shrugged his shoulders. "I'm glad it was all mental manipulation that made you think you fancied Mr Toppol."

She smiled and decided to change the subject.

"Look at the state of you, you're a right mess. Worse than usual. A severely sprained ankle and a cut in the other leg."

"Could be worse," he said shrugging his shoulders again. "Could have lost you. Besides, Sherlock Holmes wouldn't complain, so why should I?"

"Thanks, Arthur. I mean it." She kissed him on the cheek and turned to catch Lawrence up.

"I stand by what I once said."

"What?" she asked without turning round.

"That one day, Gwen Lott, I will be worthy of

you. We belong together, you and I, Gwen. I'll prove it to you one day."

She laughed gently and walked on.

Then Arthur had a deliciously wicked idea.

"Abramelin," he said.

Gwen stopped dead in her tracks, her arms flopping to her sides. Arthur's mouth went dry. Was she still under the influence of Lesta Toppol's Electromagnetic Ineffectualator?

Panting, he said, "Kiss me properly."

Gwen spun on her heels, her facial expression totally blank. She strode up to him, grabbed his head and kissed him, ramming her tongue into his mouth. Arthur felt like he was going to pass out, but willed himself not to as he didn't want to miss a moment of this succulent reward. She let him go and stared into space.

"Take your top off!" he stammered excitedly.

"In your dreams, you pervert."

She winked at him and turned to catch her brother up.

"Confounded woman," said Arthur King in his best upper-class English accent, stamping his foot. His injured foot.

He yelped and fell over. Clutching his ankle, he rolled on the ground letting forth a barrage of indecent expletives that no respectable nineteenth century gentleman sleuth would ever utter.

ABOUT THE AUTHOR

D ean Wilkinson began writing comedy in children's comics which saw him publish his own title *Fizog* – it lasted a staggering three issues. He turned his attention to telly and went on to pen episodes and sketches for many shows including *Smith & Jones*, *The Brian Conley Show*, *The Big Breakfast*, *Zig & Zag*, *Byker Grove*, *Timmy Towers*, *Comic Relief*, *Laugh Out Loud* etc. He wrote for many years for Ant and Dec, scripting series such as *The Ant And Dec Show*, *Unzipped*, *Friends Like These* and most successfully the multi-award-winning *SMTV Live*, for which he wrote *Chums*, *Cat the Dog*, *Dec Says*, *Poke-rap*, *SMTV 2099* to name just a few little gems. He is also the creator and writer of BBC TV's *Bad Penny*. Dean lives on Teesside in the north of England with his wife and daughters.

Catch up on Arthur's first adventure:

THE LEGEND OF
ARTHUR KING

"My noble lord," gasped the flabbergasted youth, "You are Arthur, King of the Britons! You are the reborn spirit of Arthur Pendragon!"

"Eh?" queried Arthur.

"You've found Excalibur! You have freed the sacred sword! You are King Arthur, you dozy twonk!"

"Oh," said Arthur dumbly. "Nice one."

A series of astounding coincidences leads 13-year-old oddball Arthur King to believe he is the reincarnation of the legendary King Arthur, once and future king of England. With his equally impressionable new friend Lawrence, Arthur finds a sword buried deep in the condemned Albion Wood and what follows is a story – nay, legend – of bravery, honour and trying to get off with his mate's older sister.

Can Arthur. . .

. . .defeat Barry "thicker than a giant's greenie" Guthries?

. . .save Albion Wood, home to a species of magical bird?

. . .win the hand of his Queen Gwen who would actually rather use that hand to punch him in the face?